BIG FISH

This Large Print Book carries the
Seal of Approval of N.A.V.H.

BIG FISH

A NOVEL OF MYTHIC PROPORTIONS

DANIEL WALLACE

Thorndike Press • Thorndike, Maine

Published in 2001 by arrangement with Algonquin Books of Chapel Hill, a division of Workman Publishing Co., Inc.

Thorndike Press Large Print Basic Series.

The tree indicium is a trademark of Thorndike Press.

The text of this Large Print edition is unabridged.
Other aspects of the book may vary from the original edition.

Set in 16 pt. Plantin by Christina S. Huff.

Printed in the United States on permanent paper.

Library of Congress Cataloging-in-Publication Data

Wallace, Daniel, 1959–
    Big fish : a novel of mythic proportions / by Daniel Wallace.
      p. cm.
    ISBN 0-7862-3043-6 (lg. print : hc : alk. paper)
    1. Fathers and sons — Fiction.   2. Terminally ill — Fiction.
    3. Storytelling — Fiction.   4. Large type books.   I. Title.
    PS3573.A4256348 B5 2001
    813′.54—dc21   00-048871

For my mother

~

In memory of my father

Acknowledgments

I have a lot of friends and family members who in one way or another helped get this book written, and I thank them all here. My gratitude extends especially to Paul Price, who has been a constant reader over the years, and Joe Regal, whose multifarious talents — agent, editor, singer, friend — make him an invaluable presence in my life. Walter Ellis and Betty Caldwell are two of the best teachers I've ever had, and without them I don't know what might have become of me. And to Kathy Pories and everyone at Algonquin, it has been a pleasure.

Contents

Part I

Part II

Part III

On one of our last car trips, near the end of my father's life as a man, we stopped by a river, and we took a walk to its banks, where we sat in the shade of an old oak tree.

After a couple of minutes my father took off his shoes and his socks and placed his feet in the clear-running water, and he looked at them there. Then he closed his eyes and smiled. I hadn't seen him smile like that in a while.

Suddenly he took a deep breath and said, "This reminds me."

And then he stopped, and thought some more. Things came slow for him then if they ever came at all, and I guessed he was thinking of some joke to tell, because he always had some joke to tell. Or he might tell me a story that would celebrate his adventurous and heroic life. And I wondered, What does this remind him of? Does it remind him of the duck in the hardware store? The horse in the bar? The boy who was knee-high to a grasshopper? Did it remind him of the dinosaur egg he found one day, then lost, or the country he once ruled for the better part of a week?

"This reminds me," he said, "of when I was a boy."

I looked at this old man, my old man with his old white feet in this clear-running stream, these

11

moments among the very last in his life, and I thought of him suddenly, and simply, as a boy, a child, a youth, with his whole life ahead of him, much as mine was ahead of me. I'd never done that before. And these images — the now and then of my father — converged, and at that moment he turned into a weird creature, wild, concurrently young and old, dying and new-born.

My father became a myth.

I

The Day He Was Born

He was born during the driest summer in forty years. The sun baked the fine red Alabama clay to a grainy dust, and there was no water for miles. Food was scarce, too. No corn or tomatoes or even squash that summer, all of it withered beneath the hazy white sky. Everything died, seemed like: chickens first, then cats, then pigs, and then dogs. Went into the stew, though, the lot, bones and all.

One man went crazy, ate rocks, and died. It took ten men to carry him to his grave he was so heavy, ten more to dig it, it was so dry.

Looking east people said, *Remember that rolling river?*

Looking west, *Remember Talbert's Pond?*

The day he was born began as just another day. The sun rose, peered down on the little wooden house where a wife, her belly as big as the country, scrambled up the last egg they had for her husband's breakfast. The husband was already out in the field, turning the dust with his plow round the black and twisted roots of some mysterious vegetable. The sun shone hard and bright.

When he came in for his egg he wiped the sweat from his brow with a ragged blue bandanna. Then he wrung the sweat from it and let it drip into an old tin cup. For something to drink, later on.

The day he was born the wife's heart stopped, briefly, and she died. Then she came back to life. She'd seen her self suspended above herself. She saw her son, too — said he glowed. When her self rejoined with herself she said she felt a warmth there.

Said, "Soon. He'll be here soon."

She was right.

The day he was born someone spotted a cloud over thataway, with something of a darkness to it. People gathered to watch. One, two, two times two, suddenly fifty people and more, all looking skyward, at this rather small cloud moving close to their parched and frazzled home place. The husband came out to look, too. And there it was: a cloud. First real cloud in weeks.

The only person in that whole town not cloud-watching was the wife. She had fallen to the floor, breathless with pain. So breathless she couldn't scream. She thought she was screaming — she had her mouth open that way — but nothing was coming out. Of her mouth. Elsewhere, though, she was busy. With him. He was coming. And where was her husband?

Out looking at a cloud.

That was some cloud, too. Not small at all, really, a respectable cloud, looming large and gray over all the dried-up acres. The husband took off his hat and squinted, taking a step down off the porch for a better look.

The cloud brought a little wind with it, too. It felt good. A little wind brushing gently across their faces felt good. And then the husband heard thunder — boom! — or so he thought. But what he heard was his wife kicking over a table with her legs. Sure sounded like thunder, though. That's what it sounded like.

He took a step farther out into the field.

"Husband!" his wife screamed then at the top of her lungs. But it was too late. Husband was too far gone and couldn't hear. He couldn't hear a thing.

The day he was born all the people of the town gathered in the field outside his house, watching the cloud. Small at first, then merely respectable, the cloud soon turned huge, whale-size at least, churning strikes of white light within it and suddenly breaking and burning the tops of pine trees and worrying some of the taller men out there;

watching, they slouched, and waited.

The day he was born things changed.

Husband became Father, Wife became Mom.

The day Edward Bloom was born, it rained.

In Which He Speaks to Animals

My father had a way with animals, everybody said so. When he was a boy, raccoons ate out of his hand. Birds perched on his shoulder as he helped his own father in the field. One night, a bear slept on the ground outside his window, and why? He knew the animals' special language. He had that quality.

Cows and horses took a peculiar liking to him as well. Followed him around et cetera. Rubbed their big brown noses against his shoulder and snorted, as if to say something specially to him.

A chicken once sat in my father's lap and laid an egg there — a little brown one. Never seen anything like it, nobody had.

The Year It Snowed in Alabama

It never snowed in Alabama and yet it snowed the winter my father was nine. It came down in successive white sheets, hardening as it fell, eventually covering the landscape in pure ice, impossible to dig out of. Caught below the snowy tempest you were doomed; above it, you merely had time to consider your doom.

Edward was a strong, quiet boy with a mind of his own, but not one to talk back to his father when a chore needed doing, a fence mended, a stray heifer lured back home. As the snow started falling that Saturday evening and on into the next morning, Edward and his father first built snowmen and snow towns and various other constructions, realizing only later that day the immensity and danger of the unabating snowfall. But it's said that my father's snowman was a full sixteen feet tall. In order to reach that height, he had engineered a device made out of pine branches and pulleys, with which he was able to move up and down at will. The snowman's eyes were made out of old wagon wheels, abandoned for years; its nose was the top of a grain silo; and its mouth — in a half-smile, as if the snowman were thinking of something warm and humorous — was the bark cut from the side of an oak tree.

His mother was inside cooking. Smoke rose from the chimney in streams of gray and white, curling into the sky. She heard a distant picking and scraping outside the door, but was too busy to pay it much mind. Didn't even look up when her husband and son came in, a half hour later, sweating in the cold.

"We've got ourselves a situation," her husband said.

"Well," she said, "tell me about it."

Meanwhile, the snow continued to fall and the door they'd just dug through to was nearly blocked again. His father took the shovel and cleared a passage again.

Edward watched — Father shovel, snow fall, Father shovel, snow fall — until the roof of the cabin itself started creaking. His mother found that a snowdrift had formed in their bedroom. They reckoned it was time they got out.

But where to? All the living world was ice now, pure white and frozen. His mother packed up the food she'd been cooking and gathered together some blankets.

They spent that night in the trees.

The next morning was a Monday. The snow stopped, the sun rose. The temperature hovered below zero.

Mother said, "About time you got off to school, isn't it Edward?"

"I guess it is," he said, no questions asked. Which is just the kind of boy he was.

After breakfast he climbed down from the tree and walked the six miles to the little schoolhouse. Saw a man frozen in a block of ice on the way there. About froze himself, too — didn't, though. He made it. He was a couple of minutes early, in fact.

And there was his schoolmaster, sitting on a wood pile, reading. All he could see of the schoolhouse was the weather vane, the rest of it buried beneath the weekend's snowfall.

"Morning, Edward," he said.

"Morning," Edward said.

And then he remembered: he'd forgotten his homework.

Went back home to get it.

True story.

His Great Promise

They say he never forgot a name or a face or your favorite color, and that by his twelfth year he knew everybody in his home town by the sound their shoes made when they walked.

They say he grew so tall so quickly that for a time — months? the better part of a year? — he was confined to his bed because the calcification of his bones could not keep up with his height's ambition, so that when he tried to stand he was like a dangling vine and would fall to the floor in a heap.

Edward Bloom used his time wisely, reading. He read almost every book there was in Ashland. A thousand books — some say ten thousand. History, Art, Philosophy. Horatio Alger. It didn't matter. He read them all. Even the telephone book.

They say that eventually he knew more than anybody, even Mr. Pinkwater, the librarian.

He was a big fish, even then.

My Father's Death: *Take 1*

It happens like this. Old Dr. Bennett, our family doctor, shuffles out of the guest room and gently shuts the door behind him. Older than old, a collection of sags and wrinkles, Dr. Bennett has been our doctor forever. He was there when I was born, cutting the cord, handing my red and shriveled body to my mother. Dr. Bennett has cured us of diseases that must number in the dozens, and he has done so with the charm and bedside manner of a physician from a bygone age, which, in effect, he is. It is this same man who is ushering my father from the world and who comes out of my father's room now and removes the stethoscope from his old ears, and looks at us, my mother and me, and shakes his head.

"There's nothing I can do," he says in his raspy voice. He wants to throw his hands in the air in exasperation but doesn't, he's too old to move that way anymore. "I'm sorry. I'm so sorry. If you have any peace to make with Edward, anything to say at all, I suggest you say it now."

We've been expecting this. My mother

grips my hand and forces a bitter smile. This has not been an easy time for her, of course. Over the past months she has dwindled in size and spirit, alive but distanced from life. Her gaze falls just short of its goal. I look at her now and she looks lost, as if she doesn't know where she is, or who she is. Our life has changed so much since Father came home to die. The process of his dying has killed us all a little bit. It's as if, instead of going to work every day, he's had to dig his own grave out back, in the lot behind the pool. And dig it not all at once, but an inch or two at a time. As if this is what made him so tired, gave him those rings beneath his eyes, and not, as Mother insisted on calling it, his "X-ray therapy." As if every evening when he returned from his digging, dirt rimming his fingernails, and sat in his chair to read the paper, he might say, *Well, it's coming along. Got another inch done today.* And my mother might say, *Did you hear that, William? Your father got another inch done today.* And I might say, *That's great, Dad, great. If there's anything I can do to help, just let me know.*

"Mom," I say.

"I'll go in first," she says, snapping to. "And then if it seems like —"

If it seems like he's going to die she'll call

for me. This is how we talk. In the land of the dying, sentences go unfinished, you know how they're going to end.

So with this she gets up and walks into the room. Dr. Bennett shakes his head, takes off his glasses and rubs them with the end of his blue-and-red-striped tie. I look at him, aghast. He is so old, so terribly old: why is my father dying before him?

"Edward Bloom," he says to no one. "Who would have thought it?"

And who would have? Death was the worst thing that ever could have happened to my father. I know how this sounds — it's the worst thing that happens to most of us — but with him it was particularly awful, especially those last few preparatory years, the growing sicknesses that disabled him in this life, even as they seemed to be priming him for the next.

Worse yet, it made him stay at home. He hated that. He hated to wake up in the same room every morning, see the same people, do the same things. Before all this he had used home as a refueling station. An itinerant dad, home for him was a stop on his way somewhere else, working toward a goal that was unclear. What drove him? It wasn't money; we had that. We had a nice house and a few cars and the pool out back; there seemed to be nothing we absolutely couldn't afford. And it wasn't for promotion — he ran his own business. It was something more than either of these things, but what, I couldn't say. It was as though he lived in a state of constant aspiration; getting there, wherever it was, wasn't the important thing: it was the battle, and the battle after that, and the war was never ending. So he worked and he worked. He was gone for weeks at a time, to places like New York or Europe or Japan, and would return at some odd hour, say nine at night, and fix a drink, reclaiming his chair and his titular position as father of the house. And he would always have some fabulous story to tell.

"In Nagoya," he said on one such night of arrival, my mother in her chair, he in his, and me on the floor at his feet, "I saw a two-headed woman. I swear to you. A beautiful two-headed Japanese woman who performed the tea ceremony with such grace and such beauty. You really couldn't tell which head was prettier."

"There's no such thing as a two-headed woman," I said.

"Really?" he said, cornering me with his eyes. "This from Mr. Teenage-Been-Around-the-World-Seen-Everything, thank you very much. I stand corrected."

"Really?" I said. "Two heads?"

"And every inch a lady," he said. "A geisha, in fact. Most of her life spent hidden away learning the complex tradition of geisha society, and rarely seen in public — which, of course, explains your skepticism. I was fortunate enough to be allowed access to the inner sanctum through a series of business friends and government contacts. I had to pretend that nothing was the least bit strange about her, of course; had I so much as raised an eyebrow, it would have been an insult of historical proportions. I simply took my tea as the rest of them did, uttering a low-pitched 'Domo,' which is Japanese for thank you."

Everything he did was without parallel.

At home, the magic of his absence yielded to the ordinariness of his presence. He drank a bit. He didn't become angry, but frustrated and lost, as though he had fallen into a hole. On those first nights home his eyes were so bright you would swear they glowed in the dark, but then after a few days his eyes became weary. He began to seem out of his element, and he suffered for it.

So he was not a good candidate for death; it made being at home even worse. He tried to make the best of it in the beginning by making long-distance calls to people in strange places all around the world, but soon he became too sick to do even that. He became just a man, a man without a job, without a story to tell, a man, I realized, I didn't know.

"You know what would be nice right now?" he says to me on this day, looking relatively well for a man who, according to Dr. Bennett, I might never see alive again. "A glass of water. Do you mind?"

"Not at all," I say.

I bring him the glass and he takes a sip or two out of it, while I hold the bottom for him so it won't spill. I smile at this guy who looks not like my father anymore but like a version of my father, one in a series, similar but different, and definitely flawed in many ways. He used to be hard to look at, all the changes he'd been through, but I've gotten used to it now. Even though he doesn't have any hair and his skin is mottled and scabbed, I'm used to it.

"I don't know if I told you this," he says, taking a breath. "But there was this panhandler who stopped me every morning when I came out of this coffee shop near the office. Every day I gave him a quarter. Every day. I mean, it became so routine the panhandler didn't even bother asking anymore — I just slipped him a quarter. Then I got sick and was out for a couple of weeks and I went back there and you know what he says to me?"

"What, Dad?"

" 'You owe me three-fifty,' he says."

"That's funny," I say.

"Well, laughter is the best medicine," he says, though neither of us is laughing. Neither of us even smiles. He just looks at me with a deepening sadness, the way it happens sometimes with him, going from one emotion to another the way some people channel surf.

"I guess it's kind of appropriate," he says. "Me using the guest room."

"How's that?" I say, though I know the answer. This is not the first time he's made mention of it, even though it was his decision to move out of the bedroom he shared with Mother. "I don't want her to go to bed every night after I'm gone looking over at my side and shivering, if you know what I mean." He somehow feels his sequestration here to be emblematic.

"Appropriate inasmuch as I'm a kind of guest," he says, looking around the oddly formal room. My mother always felt that guests had to have things just so, so she made the room look as much like a hotel as possible. You've got your little chair, bedside table, harmless oil reproduction by some Old Master hanging above the chest of drawers. "I haven't really been around here so much, you know. At home. Not as much as we all would have liked. Look at you, you're a grown man and I — I completely missed it." He swallows, which for him is a real workout. "I wasn't there for you, was I, son?"

"No," I say, perhaps too quickly but with as much kindness as the word can possibly hold.

"Hey," he says, after which he coughs for a bit. "Don't hold back or anything, just 'cause I'm, you know."

"Don't worry."

"The truth and nothing but the truth."

"So help me —"

"God. Fred. Whoever."

He takes another sip of water. It seems not to be a matter of thirst so much as it is a desire for this element, to feel it on his tongue, his lips: he loves the water. Once upon a time he swam.

"But you know, my father was gone a lot, too," he says, his voice crackling soft. "So I know what it's like. My dad was a farmer. I told you that, didn't I? I remember once he had to go off somewhere to get a special kind of seed to plant in the fields. Hopped a freight. Said he'd be back that night. One thing and another happened and he couldn't get off. Rode it all the way out to California. Gone most of the spring. Planting time came and went. But when he came back he had the most marvelous seeds."

"Let me guess," I say. "He planted them and a huge vine grew up into the clouds, and at the top of the clouds was a castle, where a giant lived."

"How did you know?"

"And a two-headed woman who served him tea, no doubt."

At this my father tweaks his eyebrows and smiles, for a moment deep in pleasure.

"You remember," he says.

"Sure."

"Remembering a man's stories makes him immortal, did you know that?"

I shake my head.

"It does. You never really believed that one though, did you?"

"Does it matter?"

He looks at me.

"No," he says. Then, "Yes. I don't know. At least you remembered. The point is, I think — the point is I tried to get home more. I did. Things happened, though. Natural disasters. The earth split once I think, the sky opened several times. Sometimes I barely made it out alive."

His old scaly hand crawls over to touch my knee. His fingers are white, the nails cracking and dull, like old silver.

"I'd say I'd missed you," I say, "if I knew what I was missing."

"I'll tell you what the problem was," he says, lifting his hand from my knee and motioning for me to come closer. And I do. I want to hear. The next word could be his last.

"I wanted to be a great man," he whispers.

"Really?" I say, as if this comes as some sort of surprise to me.

"Really," he says. His words come slow and weak but steady and strong in feeling and thought. "Can you believe it? I thought it was my destiny. A big fish in a big pond — that's what I wanted. That's what I wanted from day one. I started small. For a long time I worked for other people. Then I started my own business. I got these molds and I made candles in the basement. That business failed. I sold baby's breath to floral shops. That failed. Finally, though, I got into import/export and everything took off. I had dinner with a prime minister once, William. A prime minister! Can you imagine, this boy from Ashland having dinner in the same room with a —. There's not a continent I haven't set foot on. Not one. There are seven of them, right? I'm starting to forget which ones I . . . never mind. Now all that seems so unimportant, you know? I mean, I don't even know what a great man *is* anymore — the, uh, prerequisites. Do you, William?"

"Do I what?"

"Know," he says. "Know what makes a man great."

I think about this for a long time, secretly hoping he forgets he ever asked the question. His mind has a way of wandering, but something in the way he looks at me says he's not forgetting anything now, he's holding on tight to that thought, and he's waiting for my answer. I don't know what makes a man great. I've never thought about it before. But at a time like this "I don't know" just won't do. This is an occasion one rises to, and so I make myself as light as possible and wait for a lift.

"I think," I say after a while, waiting for the right words to come, "that if a man could be said to be loved by his son, then I think that man could be considered great."

For this is the only power I have, to bestow upon my father the mantle of greatness, a thing he sought in the wider world, but one that, in a surprise turn of events, was here at home all along.

"Ah," he says, "*those* parameters," he says, stumbling over the word, all of a sudden seeming slightly woozy. "Never thought about it in those terms, exactly. Now that we are, though, thinking about it like that, I mean, in this case," he says, "in this very specific case, *mine* —"

"Yeah," I say. "You are hereby and forever after my father, Edward Bloom, a Very Great Man. So help you Fred."

And in lieu of a sword I touch him once, gently, on the shoulder.

With these words he seems to rest. His eyes close heavily, and with an eerie sort of finality that I recognize as the beginning of a departure. When the window curtains part as though of their own accord I believe for a moment that this must be the passage of his spirit going from this world to the next. But it's only the central air coming on.

"About that two-headed lady," he says with his eyes closed, murmuring, as if falling into a sleep.

"I've *heard* about the two-headed lady," I say, shaking him gently by the shoulder. "I don't want to hear about her anymore, Dad. Okay?"

"I wasn't going to *tell* you about the two-headed lady, Mr. Smarty-pants," he says.

"You weren't?"

"I was going to tell you about her sister."

"She had a *sister?*"

"Hey," he says, opening his eyes now, getting his second wind. "Would I kid you about something like that?"

The Girl in the River

Near the banks of the Blue River was an oak tree where my father used to stop and rest. The tree spread its branches wide, providing shade, and around its base was a soft, cool green moss, on which he would lay his head and sometimes sleep, the river soothing him with its smooth sounds. It's here he came one day, and as he was drifting off into a dream woke to see a beautiful young woman bathing in the river. Her long hair shone like gold itself and curled to her bare shoulders. Her breasts were small and round. Cupping the cool water in her hands, she let it run down her face, her chest, and back into the river.

Edward tried to remain calm. He kept telling himself, *Don't move. If you move an inch she'll see you.* He didn't want to scare her. And, honestly, he had never glimpsed a woman in her natural state before, and wanted to study her a little longer before she left him.

That's when he saw the snake. Cottonmouth, had to be. Making a little break in the water as it glided toward her, its small reptilian head angling for flesh. Hard to believe a snake that size could kill you, but it could. A snake that size killed Calvin Bryant. It bit him on the ankle and seconds later he was dead. Calvin Bryant was two times bigger than her.

So there was no real decision to be made. My father relied on instinct and dove head first into the river, hands outstretched, just as the cottonmouth was getting set to place his two small fangs into her small waist. She screamed, of course. A man coming at you, diving into the water — you bet she screamed. And he rose out of the water with that snake writhing in his hands, mouth searching for something to lay into, and she screamed again. Finally he was able to wrap the snake up in his shirt. Didn't believe in killing, my dad. He'd take it to a friend who collected snakes.

Here's the scene now, though: a young man and a young woman both standing waist deep in the Blue River with their shirts off, looking at each other. Sun breaking through in places, shining, glinting off the water. But these two mostly in shadow. One studying the other. All quiet except for the nature around them. Hard to talk now because what do you say? *My name is Edward, what's yours?* You don't say that. You say what she said, the moment she was able to speak.

"You saved my life."

And he had, hadn't he? She was about to get bitten by a poisonous snake and he had saved her. Risked his own life to do it, too. Though neither of them mentioned that. Didn't have to. They both knew it.

"You're brave," she said.

"No ma'am," he said, though she couldn't have been much older than he. "I just saw you, and I saw that snake, and I — I jumped."

"What's your name?"

"Edward," he said.

"Okay, Edward. From now on this is your place. We'll call it . . . Edward's Grove. The tree, this part of the river, this water, everything. And whenever you're not feeling good or need something to happen, you come down here and just rest, and think about it."

"Okay," he said, though he would have said okay to about anything then. Though way above water, his head was swimming. He felt as though he had left this world for a brief time. Hadn't come back yet.

She smiled.

"Now you turn around," she said, "and I'll get dressed."

"Okay."

And he turned around, flushed with an almost intolerable good feeling. So good he could hardly stand it. As though he'd been made over, better, and all new.

He didn't know how long it might take a woman to dress, so he gave her a full five minutes. And when he turned around of course she was gone — vanished. Hadn't heard her go but she was gone. He might have called after her — would've liked to — but he didn't know what to call. Wished he'd asked now, first thing.

The wind blew through the oak tree, and the water ran its course. And she was gone. And in his shirt no snake at all, but a stick. A small brown stick.

It looked like a snake, though — it did. Especially when he threw it in the river and watched it swim away.

His Quiet Charm

They say he had a special charm, a flair for understatement, a knack for a sudden thoughtfulness. He was — shy. Still: sought out, my father, by women. Call it a quiet charm. He was quite handsome, too, though he never let this go to his head. He was a friend to all, and everybody was his friend.

They say he was funny, even then. They say he knew a few good jokes. Not in large groups, where he'd keep to himself, but get him alone — as many female Ashlanders apparently tried to do! — and he could really make you laugh. They say you could hear them laughing into the night, my father and these sweet young girls, hear their laughter echoing through town in the night, on his front porch, swinging. Laughter was the sound of choice to sleep by in Ashland. That's the way it was, back then.

How He Tamed the Giant

My father's youthful exploits were many, and the stories told even to this day are beyond counting. But perhaps his most formidable task was facing Karl, the Giant, for in doing so he was risking his very life. Karl was as tall as any two men, as wide as any three, and as strong as any ten. His face and arms bore the scars of a life lived brutally, a life closer to that of animals than of men. And such was his demeanor. They say Karl was born of woman like any mortal, but it became clear soon enough that a mistake had been made. He was just too huge. His mother would buy him clothes in the morning, and by afternoon the seams would tear, so fast was his body growing. At night he'd go to sleep in a bed made to his size by a woodsman, and by morning his feet would be hanging over the edge. And he was eating constantly! It didn't matter how much food she bought or produced from her own fields: her cupboards were always bare by nightfall, and still he complained of an empty stomach. His great fist pounded the table for more food — "Now!" he screamed. "Mother, now!" After fourteen years of this she could no longer stand it, and one day while Karl's face was buried in a side of venison she packed her bags and left by the backdoor, never to return; her absence went unnoticed until the food was gone. Then he became bitter and angry and — most of all — hungry.

This is when he came to Ashland. At night, while the townsfolk slept, Karl crept through the yards and gardens in search of food. In the beginning, he took only what they grew there; morning would come and the people of Ashland would find whole cornfields ravaged, their apple trees bare, the water tower dry. No one knew what to do. Karl, having grown too large for it, had moved from his home into the mountains surrounding town. Who cared to face him in such terrain? And what would they do, these people, before the ghastly monstrosity Karl had become?

This pillaging went on for some time, until one day half a dozen dogs came up missing. It seemed the very life of the town was threatened. Something had to be done — but what?

My father came up with a plan. It was dangerous, but there seemed to be nothing else to do, and with the blessing of the town one fine summer morning father set out on his way. He headed for the mountains, where he knew of a cave. This is where he thought Karl lived.

The cave was hidden behind a stand of pine and a great pile of stones, and my father knew of it from having rescued a young girl who had wandered into its depths many years ago. He stood before the cave and shouted.

"Karl!"

He heard his voice come back to him in an echo.

"Show yourself! I know you're in there. I have come with a message from our town."

Moments passed in the silence of the deep woods before my father heard a rustling, and a tremor seemed to move the earth itself. Then from the darkness of the cave rose Karl. He was bigger even than my father had dared to dream. And oh, but his was a grisly visage! Covered in cuts and bruises from living in the wild — and being so hungry at times that he didn't wait for his food to die, and sometimes his food fought back. His black hair was long and full of grease, his thick and tangled beard full of food as well as the soft and spineless crawly bugs that dined there on his crumbs.

When he saw my father he began to laugh.

"What is it *you* want, little person?" he

44

said with a terrible grin.

"You must stop coming into Ashland for your food," my father said. "Our farmers are losing their crops, and the children miss their dogs."

"What? And *you* intend to stop me?" he said, his voice booming through the valleys, no doubt all the way back to Ashland itself. "Why, I could *snap* you in my hands like a branch off a tree!"

And to demonstrate he grabbed the branch of a nearby pine and ground it to dust in his fingers.

"Why," he went on, "I could eat you and be done with you in a moment! I could!"

"And that is why I have come," my father said.

Karl's face twitched then, either from confusion or from one of the bugs that had crawled from his beard and up his cheek.

"What do you mean, that's why you've come?"

"For you to eat me," he said. "I am the first sacrifice."

"The first . . . sacrifice?"

"To you, O great Karl! We submit to your power. In order to save the many, we realize we must sacrifice a few. That makes me — what? — lunch?"

Karl seemed confounded by my father's

words. He shook his head to clear it, and a dozen creeping bugs flew from his beard and fell to the ground. His body began to shake, and for a moment he appeared about to fall, and had to right himself by leaning against the mountain wall.

It was as if he had been struck by a weapon of some kind. It was as if he had been wounded in battle.

"I . . ." he said quite softly, even sadly. "I don't want to eat you."

"You don't?" my father said, greatly relieved.

"No," Karl said. "I don't want to eat anybody," and a giant tear rolled down his beaten face. "I just get so *hungry*," he said. "My mother used to cook the most wonderful meals, but then she left, and I didn't know what to do. The dogs — I'm sorry about the dogs. I'm sorry about everything."

"I understand," my father said.

"I don't know what to do now," Karl said. "Look at me — I'm huge! I have to eat to live. But I'm all on my own now, and I don't know how to —"

"Cook," my father said. "Grow food. Tend animals."

"Exactly," Karl said. "I suppose I should just wander into the back of this cave and never come out. I've caused you too much trouble."

"We could teach you," my father said.

It took Karl a moment to understand my father's words.

"Teach me what?"

"To cook, grow food. There are acres and acres of fields here."

"You mean, I could become a farmer?"

"Yes," my father said. "You could."

And this is exactly what happened. Karl became the biggest farmer in Ashland, but my father's legend became even bigger. It was said he could charm anyone, just by walking through the room. It was said he was blessed with a special power. But my father was humble, and he said it wasn't that at all. He just liked people, and people liked him. It was that simple, he said.

In Which He Goes Fishing

Then came the flood, but what can I add to what has already been written? Rain, waves of rain, unceasing. Streams became rivers, rivers lakes, and all the lakes, growing beyond their banks, became one. Somehow, Ashland — most of it — was spared. The felicitous congruence of a mountain range, some say, parting the waters around the town. True, one corner of Ashland, houses and all, are still at the bottom of what is now called — appropriately if not very imaginatively — Big Lake, and the ghosts of those who died in the flood can still be heard on a summer night. But what is most remarkable about the lake is the catfish. Catfish as big as a man, they say — some bigger. Take your leg off if you swim too deep. Leg and more sometimes, if you don't watch out.

Only a fool or a hero would try to catch a fish that size, and my father, well — I guess he was a little of both.

He went by himself one morning at dawn and took a boat out toward the middle, deepest part of Big Lake. For bait? A mouse, deceased, found in the corncrib. He hooked it up and let her fly. It took a good five minutes to hit bottom, then he brought her up slow. Soon he got a strike. The strike took the mouse, the hook, everything. So he tried again. A bigger hook this time, stronger line, more sumptuous-looking dead mouse, and cast. The water was beginning to roil about now, roil and bubble and wave, as if the spirit of the lake was rising. Edward just kept fishing, just fishing. Maybe that was a bad idea, though, seeing how things were getting very unlakelike now. And scary. Maybe he'd reel in his little mouse and row on home. Okay then. Only, as he reels he notices the line's not moving so much as he is. Forward. And the faster he reels, the faster he moves. What he should do, he knows, is simple: let go of the pole. Let it go! Throw it in and kiss it good-bye. Who knows what's on the other end of that line, pulling him? But he can't throw it in. Can't do it. His hands in fact feel like they're a part of the pole itself. So he does the second best thing and stops reeling, but the second best thing doesn't work either: he keeps moving forward, Edward does, and fast, faster than before. This is no log then, is it? He's being pulled by a thing, a living thing — a catfish. Dolphinlike, he watches as it arcs out of the water, catching a ray from the sun as it does, beautiful, monstrous, scary — six, seven feet long? — and taking Edward with it now as it submerges, popping him right out of his boat and pulling him under and down, deep into the watery graveyard of Big Lake itself. And there he sees the homes and the farms, the fields and the roads, that small corner of Ashland that was covered over in the flood. And he sees the people, too: there's Homer Kittridge and his wife, Marla. There's Vern Talbot and Carol Smith. Homer's taking a bucket full of feed to his horses, and Carol's talking to Marla about corn. Vern's working on the tractor. Beneath fathoms and fathoms of a shadowy green water they move as if in slow motion, and when they talk little bubbles leave their lips and rise to the surface. As the catfish carries Edward swiftly by, Homer smiles and begins to wave — Edward knew Homer — but can't quite finish the gesture before they're gone again, fish and man, up and suddenly out of the water, where Edward is thrown, poleless now, to shore.

He never told anybody about this. He couldn't. Because who'd believe him? Questioned about loss of pole and boat, Edward said he fell asleep dreaming on the banks of Big Lake and they just . . . drifted away.

The Day He Left Ashland

And so it was, in roughly just this way, that Edward Bloom became a man. He was healthy, and strong, and loved by his parents. He was also a high school graduate. In the verdant fields of Ashland he ran with his companions, and with gusto he ate and drank. It was life spent as if in a dream. Only one morning he woke and knew in his heart that he must go, and he told his mother and his father, and they didn't try to stop him. But they looked at each other with foreboding, because they knew there was but one road out of Ashland, and to leave by it meant passing through the place that had no name. Those who were meant to leave Ashland passed through this place unharmed, but those who weren't stayed there forever, unable to go forward or move back. And so they said good-bye to their son knowing they might never see him again, and he the same.

The morning of the day he left was a bright one, but as he made his way toward the place that had no name the day grew dark, and the skies lowered, and a thick fog embraced him. Soon he arrived at a place much like Ashland itself, though different in important ways. On Main Street there was a bank, Cole's Pharmacy, the Christian Bookstore, Talbot's Five and Dime, Prickett's Place, Fine Jewels and Watches, the Good Food Cafe, a pool hall, a movie theater, an empty lot, a hardware store, and a grocery store, too, shelves stocked with items predating his birth. Some of the same stores were on Main Street in Ashland, but here they were empty and dark, and the windows were cracked, and the owners stared dully from the empty doorways. But they smiled when they saw my father. They smiled and waved. *A customer!* they thought. There was also a whorehouse on Main Street, right at the end there, but it wasn't like a whorehouse in the city. It was just a house where a whore lived.

As he wandered into town the people there ran to meet him, and they stared at his handsome hands.

Leaving? they asked him. *Leaving Ashland?*

They were a strange lot. One man had a shrunken arm. His right hand hung from his elbow, and the arm above the elbow was withered. His hand just peeked out of his sleeve, like a cat's head peeking out of a paper bag. One summer years ago he had been riding in a car with his arm stretched out the window, feeling the wind. But the car was running too close to the side of the road, and instead of the wind he felt the sudden sting of a telephone pole. Every bone in his lower arm was broken. His hand hung there now, useless, getting smaller and smaller with time. He welcomed my father with a smile.

Then there was a woman, in her mid-fifties about, who in almost every respect was perfectly normal. But this was the way with these people: in so many respects they were normal, there was just that *one thing*, that one terrible thing. Several years ago she'd come home from work to find her husband hanging from a water pipe in the basement. Suffered a stroke seeing him there, and as a consequence the left side of her face had been forever frozen: her lips sloped downward in the exaggerated form of a frown, the flesh around her eye sagging. She couldn't move that side of her face at all, and so when she spoke only one side of her mouth opened, and her voice sounded trapped deep inside her throat. Words climbed her throat painfully in order to escape. She had tried to leave Ashland after these things happened, but this was as far as she got.

And there were still others simply born the way they were, whose births had been the first, and worst, accidents. There was a hydrocephalic named Bert; he worked as a sweeper. Everywhere he went he carried a broom. He was the whore's son, and a problem to the men of this place: most of them had been to see the whore, and any one of them could have been the boy's father. As far as she was concerned, they all were. She had never wanted to be a whore. The town had needed one, she had been forced into the position, and over the years she became bitter. Especially after the birth of her son, she began to hate her customers. He was a great joy but a greater burden. He had no memory to speak of. He would often ask her, "Where's my daddy?" and she would aimlessly point out the window at the first man she saw. "There's your daddy," she'd tell him. He'd run outside and throw his arms around the man's neck. The next day he'd remember nothing about it, though, and he'd ask her, "Where's my daddy?" and he'd get another one, just like that.

Finally, my father met a man named Willie. He had been sitting on a bench and stood when Edward walked up, as if he'd been waiting for him. The edges of his lips were dried and cracked. His hair was gray and bristly and his eyes were small and black. He'd lost three of his fingers (two on one hand, one on the other), and he was old.

He was so old that he seemed to have gone as far forward in time as a human possibly could, and, as he was still alive, had started the trip backward. He was shrinking. He was becoming small like a baby. He moved slowly, as though he were walking knee-deep through water, and he looked at my father with a grim smile.

"Welcome to our town," he said to him, in a friendly if somewhat tired way. "Mind if I show you around?"

"I can't stay," my father said. "I'm just passing through."

"That's what they all say," Willie said as he took my father by the arm, and together they began to walk.

"Anyway," he continued, "what's your hurry? You should at least have a look at all we have to offer. Here we have a store, a nice little store, and here — over here," he said, "we have a place to go if you want to shoot the pool. Billiards, you know. You might like that."

"Thank you," Edward said, because he did not want to anger this Willie, or any of the others who were watching them. Already they had attracted a small crowd of three or four people who were following them through the otherwise empty streets, keeping their distance but leering in a wanting kind of way. "Thank you very much."

Willie's grip grew stronger still as he showed him the pharmacy, and the Christian Bookstore, and then, winking slyly, the house where the whore lived.

"She's sweet, too," Willie said. And then, as if remembering something he hadn't meant to, said, "Sometimes."

The sky was darker now, and a light rain began to fall. Willie looked up and let the water fall into his eyes. My father wiped his face and grimaced.

"We have our share of rain," Willie said, "but you get used to it."

"Everything here seems sort of . . . damp," my father said.

Willie cut him a glance.

"You get used to it," he said. "That's what this place is all about, Edward. Getting used to things."

"It's not what I want," he said.

"That, too," he said. "You get used to that, too."

They walked on in silence through the fog that gathered around their feet, through the rain that fell softly on their heads and shoulders, through the dusklike morning of this strange town. People gathered on the corners to watch them pass, some of them joining the contingent that followed. Edward caught the gaze of a gaunt man in a ragged black suit, and recognized him. It was Norther Winslow, the poet. He had left Ashland just a few years ago to go to Paris, to write. He stood looking at Edward and almost smiled, but then Edward caught sight of his right hand, which was missing two of its fingers, and Norther's face turned pallid, and clutching his hand to his chest he disappeared around a corner. People had put a lot of hope in Norther.

"Sure," Willie said, seeing what had just happened. "People like you come through here all the time."

"What do you mean?" my father said.

"Normal people," Willie said, which seemed to leave a bad taste. He spit. "Normal people and their plans. This rain, this dampness — it's a kind of residue. The residue of a dream. Of a lot of dreams, actually. Mine and his and yours."

"Not mine," Edward said.

"No," Willie said. "Not yet."

And it was then they saw the dog. It moved as an indefinite black shape through the fog until its figure emerged before them. There were spots of white on its chest and brown around its toes, but the rest of it was black. It had short, bristly hair, and seemed to be of no specific breed — a generic dog, with pieces of many dogs inside it. It was coming toward them, slowly but directly, not even stopping to smell a hydrant or a pole, not wandering, but walking. This dog was going somewhere. This dog had a destination: my father.

"What's this?" Edward said.

Willie smiled.

"A dog," Willie said. "Comes to check everybody out sooner or later, usually sooner. He's a kind of gatekeeper, if you know what I mean."

"No," my father said. "I don't know what you mean."

"You will," Willie said. "You will. Call him," he said.

"Call? What's his name?"

"No name. He never belonged to anybody so he never got a name. Just call him Dog."

"Dog."

"That's right: Dog."

So my father kneeled and clapped his hands and tried to look friendly.

"Here Dog! C'mere buddy! Here boy. Come on!"

And Dog, who had been walking a long, straight line, froze, and stared at my father for a long time — a long time for a dog, anyway. Half a minute. The hair on his back stood ridged. His eyes locked on my father's eyes. He opened his mouth and showed him his teeth and the ferocious pinkness of his gums. He was about ten feet away and growling wildly.

"Maybe I should get out of his way," he said. "I don't think he's taking to me so well."

"Stick out your hand," Willie said.

My father said, "What?"

Dog's growl came on stronger then.

"Stick out your hand and let him smell it."

"Willie, I don't think —"

"Stick out your hand," he said.

Slowly, my father stuck out his hand. Dog came to it with his slow steps, his low snarl, his jaws set to snap. But as the tip of his nose rubbed against my father's knuckles he whined, and Dog licked my father's whole hand. Dog's tail wagged. My father's heart: beating.

Willie looked on in sadness and defeat, as if he had been betrayed.

"Does this mean I can go?" my father asked, standing, while the dog rubbed against his legs.

"Not yet," Willie said, grabbing my father again, the grip of his hand pinching deep into the muscle. "You'll want a cup of coffee before you go."

★ ★ ★

The Good Food Cafe was one big room lined with green vinyl booths and gold-speckled Formica tables. There were paper placemats on the tables and thin silver spoons and forks, encrusted with dried food. There was a dimness inside, a thick grayness, and though almost every table was occupied, there seemed to be no real life here, none of the anxious expectancy of a hunger about to be sated. But when Willie and my father came in they all looked up and smiled, as though their meal had just arrived.

Willie and my father sat at a table and without even asking were brought two cups of coffee by a silent waitress. Deep black steaming pools. Willie stared into his cup and shook his head.

"You think you've got it made, don't you, son?" Willie smiled as he brought the coffee to his lips. "Think you're a real big fish. But you're not the first we've seen. Look at Jimmy Edwards over there. Big football star. Good student. He wanted to be a businessman in the city, make his fortune, whatnot. Never made it out of here, though. Didn't have the intestinal fortitude, you know." He leaned over and whispered. "That dog got his left index finger."

My father looked and saw it was true. Jimmy moved his hand slowly off the table, and stuck it in his pocket, and turned away. My father looked at the others, who were looking at him, and saw that it was the same with everybody. Nobody could claim all their fingers, and some could only boast a few. My father looked at Willie, about to ask him why. But it was as if Willie could read his mind.

"The number of times they tried to go," he said. "Either out of here or back to where they came from. That dog," he said, looking at his own hand, "don't play games."

Then, slowly, as if drawn there by a sound only they could hear, the people sitting at the tables around him stood and walked to the edge of his booth, where they looked at him and smiled. Some of their names he remembered from his childhood in Ashland. Cedric Fowlkes, Sally Dumas, Ben Lightfoot. But they were different now. He could almost see through them, seemed like, but then something happened and he couldn't, as if they were coming in and out of focus.

He looked beyond them to the door of the cafe, where Dog sat. Dog sat there staring in, unmoving, and my father rubbed his hands together, wondering what he was waiting on, and if he had missed his chance to get by Dog before and the next time maybe he wouldn't be so lucky.

A woman named Rosemary Wilcox stood by the booth. She had fallen in love with a man from the city and tried to run off with him, but only he had made it out. Her eyes were dark and sunken into what was once a pretty face. She remembered my father from when he was little, and told him how nice it was to see him again, so big and tall and handsome.

The crowd around the booth grew larger, and moved in closer, and my father found he couldn't move. There was no space for it. Crowding up close beside him at the edge of the booth was a man older even than Willie. He was like petrified life. His skin had dried and grown tight around his bones, and his veins were blue and as cold-looking as a frozen river.

"I — I wouldn't trust that dog," the man said slowly. "I just wouldn't take the chance, son. He didn't get you before but you never know about the next time. S'unpredictable. So sit tight," he said, "and tell us all about the world you want to go to, and the things you want to find there."

And the old man closed his eyes, and so did Willie, and so did they all, all of them wanting to hear about the bright world my father knew was waiting for him just around the bend, on the other side of this dark place. And so he told them, and when he finished they all thanked him and smiled.

And the old man said, "That was nice."

"Can we do it again tomorrow?" someone said.

"Let's do it again tomorrow," another whispered.

"It's good to have you," a man said to my father. "Good to have you here."

"I know a real nice girl," Rosemary said. "Pretty, too. Looks like me a little bit. I'd be happy to get you two together, if you know what I mean."

"I'm sorry," my father said, looking from one to the other. "There's been a misunderstanding. I'm not here to stay."

"I reckon there has been a misunderstanding," Ben Lightfoot said, looking at my father with a deep loathing.

"But we can't let you go," Rosemary said, in a soft voice.

"I *have* to go," my father said, trying to stand. But he couldn't, they crowded round him so.

"At least stay for a little while," Willie said. "A few days at least."

"Get to know us," Rosemary said, brushing her hair from her eyes with her terrible hand.

"You'll forget about the rest."

But suddenly there came a rustling sound from the back of the circle of men and women around him and then a scream, and a barking growl, and like a miracle the people moved away. It was Dog. He growled a vicious growl, and showed them his terrible teeth, and they all backed away from the drooling monster, clutching their hands close to their chests. My father took his chance and ran through the opening and he didn't look back. He ran through the darkness until it became light again, and the world turned green and wonderful. The asphalt gave way to gravel, the gravel to dirt, and the beauty of a magic world seemed not too far away. When the road ended he stopped and breathed and found that Dog was right behind him, tongue lolling, and when he reached my father, he rubbed his warm body against his legs. There was no sound now save the wind through the trees and their feet along a barely beaten trail. And then all at once the woods opened up, and before them was a lake, a huge green lake bending off into the distance as far as he could see, and at the edge of the lake was a small wooden dock, bobbing in the waves the wind made. They made their way down to it, and once there Dog collapsed, as if emptied of all strength. My father looked around him, proud somehow, and he watched the sun set behind the stand of trees, and he breathed in the air, and he dug his fingers into the loose skin around Dog's warm neck, rubbing the muscles there with a thorough gentleness, as though he were rubbing the muscles of his own heart, and Dog made his dog-happy sounds. And the sun set, and the moon rose, and the water in the lake began to gently ripple, and in the white light of the moon then he saw the girl, her head breaking the surface a good ways out, the water flowing through her hair and back into the lake, and she was smiling. She was smiling, and my father was, too. And then she waved. She waved at my father, and he waved back.

"Hello!" he said, waving to her. "Good-bye!"

Entering a New World

The story of my father's first day in the world he would come to live in is best told perhaps by a man who worked with him, Jasper "Buddy" Barron. Buddy was vice president of Bloom Inc., taking over the helm when my father retired.

Buddy was a natty dresser. He wore a power-yellow tie, an executive's dark blue pinstripe suit, black shoes, and those tight, thin, almost transparent socks, in the same blue hue of his suit, that climbed to an undetermined length up his calves. He had a silk handkerchief peering like a pet mouse over the edge of the false pocket on the heart side of his suit. And he was the first and only man I've ever met who actually had graying temples, just like they say in books. The rest of his hair was dark and full and healthy, and his part was one long straight line of pinkish scalp, a country road across his head.

When he told this story he liked to lean back in his chair and smile.

"The year was nineteensomething or other," he'd begin. "Longer ago than any of us want to remember. Edward had just left home. Seventeen years old. For the first time in his life he was on his own, but was he worried? No, he wasn't worried: his mother had given him a few dollars to live on — ten, maybe twelve — more money, at any rate, than he had ever had in his life. And he had his dreams. Dreams are what keep a man going, William, and already your father was dreaming empire. But looking at him on the day he left that town he was born in, you would have seen little more than a young, handsome boy with nothing but the clothes on his back and the holes in his shoes. You might not have actually seen the holes in his shoes, but they were there, William; the holes were there.

"That first day he walked thirty miles. That night, he slept under the stars on a bed of pine straw. And here, on this night, is where fate's hand first tugged on your father's belt loops. For as he slept he was come upon by two men-of-the-woods, who beat him within an inch of his life and took from him every last dollar he had. He barely survived, and yet thirty years later when he first told me this story — and this to me is vintage Edward Bloom — he said that if he ever met with those men again, the two thugs who beat him within an inch of his life and took his last dollar, he would thank them —

thank them — for, in a way, they determined the course of the rest of his life.

"At the time, of course, dying in the dark of that strange wood, he was far from grateful. But by morning he was well rested, and, though bleeding still from various parts of his body, he began walking, no longer knowing or caring where he was going, but just walking, forward, onward, ready for whatever Life and Fate chose to hurl at him next — when he saw an old country store, and an old man out in front of it, rocking back and forth in his chair, back and forth, forth and back, who presently began to stare with alarm at the bloody figure approaching. He called for his wife, and she called for her daughter, and within half a minute they had a pot of hot water, a washcloth, and a bunch of bandages made from a sheet they had just torn into strips, and stood ready as Edward hobbled to meet them. They were ready to save this stranger's life. More than ready: they were determined.

"But of course, he wouldn't let them. He could not let them save his life. No man of your father's integrity — and they are few, William, they are a precious few and far between — would accept such charity, even when it was a matter of life or death. For how could he live with himself, if indeed he did live at all, knowing that his life was so inextricably bound to others, knowing that he was not his own man?

"So, still bleeding, and with one of his legs broken in two places, Edward found a broom and swept the store clean. Then he found a mop and a pail, for in his haste to do the right thing he had completely forgotten his open, profusely bleeding wounds, and didn't realize until he had finished sweeping that he had left a trail of his own blood throughout the entire store. So he mopped. He scoured. He got on his knees with a rag and scrubbed as the old man, the wife, and child watched him. They were in awe. They were awestruck. They were watching a man trying to remove his own blood stains from a pine wood floor. It was impossible, impossible — yet he tried. That's the thing, William: he tried, tried until he could try no more, until he fell on his face flat out, still clutching the rag — dead.

"Or so they thought. They thought he had died. They rushed to his body: there was some life in him yet. And in a scene, as your father described it, that has always reminded me somehow of Michelangelo's *Pieta*, the mother, a strong woman, lifted him up and held him in her arms, in her lap, this young man, this dying man, praying for his life. It seemed hopeless. But as the others anxiously crowded around him, he opened his eyes and said what might have been his last words, said to the old man whose store Edward had immediately realized was empty of customers, said in what might have been his last breath, *'Advertise.'*"

Buddy would let the word ring through the room.

"And the rest, as they say, is history. Your father recovered. Soon he was strong again. He plowed the fields, weeded the gardens, helped around the store. He roamed about the countryside posting little notices, advertising for Ben Jimson's Country Store. It was his idea to call it a 'country' store, by the way. He thought it sounded more friendly, more appealing than just 'store,' and he was right. It was also at this time your father invented the slogan 'Buy one, get one free.' Five little words, William, but they turned Ben Jimson into a rich man.

"He stayed with the Jimsons for almost a year, earning his first little nest egg. The world, like a splendid flower, opened up for him. And as you can see," he would say, gesturing to the gold and leather extravagancies of his own office, and with a minor nod in my direction, as though I, too, were nothing but a product of my father's legendary industriousness, "for a boy from Ashland, Alabama, he's done rather well."

II

The Old Lady and the Eye

After leaving the Jimsons my father wandered south through the countryside, going from town to town, having many adventures, and meeting a number of interesting and fantastic people. But there was an aim to his wandering, a purpose, as there was to everything he did. He had learned many of life's lessons in the past year, and now hoped to expand his understanding of the nature of the world even more by attending a college. He heard of a city called Auburn where such a college existed. It was to this town he traveled.

He arrived there of an evening, tired and hungry, and found a room in the home of an old woman who took in borders. She fed him and gave him a bed in which to rest. He slept for three days and three nights, and when he awoke felt strong again, clear in mind and body. Thereupon he thanked the old woman for her assistance, and in return offered to help her in any way he could.

Well, it so happened the old woman had only one eye. The other eye, which was made of glass, she took out every night and soaked in a cup of water on the nightstand beside her bed.

And it so happened that, some days before my father arrived, a group of youths had broken into the old woman's home and stolen her eye, so she told my father that she would be grateful if he could but find her eye and return it to her. My father made a vow then and there that he would do it, and he left her home in search of the eye that very morning.

The day was cool and bright, and my father full of hope.

The city of Auburn was named after a poem, and it was, at that time, a great center of learning. Young people eager to know the secrets of the world crowded into small classrooms, alert to the words of the peripatetic professor before them. This is where Edward longed to be.

On the other hand, many came there merely to fool around, and organized in large groups for this purpose alone. It didn't take long for my father to learn that it was one of these groups that had broken into the old woman's home and stolen her eye.

Indeed, the eye had become the focus of some notoriety, and was discussed openly and with great veneration among certain individuals Edward Bloom shrewdly befriended.

It was said the eye had magic powers.

It was said the eye could see.

It was said to be bad luck to look directly into the eye, for the old woman would know you then, and on a dark night she would hunt you down and find you, and then she would do unspeakable things to you.

The eye never stayed in the same place twice. Each night it was given to a different boy as a rite of initiation. It was the boy's duty to see that no harm came to the eye. All that night the boy possessing the eye wasn't allowed to sleep; he could only watch the eye. The eye was wrapped in a soft red cloth, and the cloth was placed inside a small wooden box. In the morning, the eye was returned to the leader of the group who asked the boy questions, and who examined the eye and then sent him on his way.

All this Edward learned in a short time.

In order to return the eye to the old woman, Edward realized, he would have to become one of the boys who possessed it for the night. This is what he sought to do.

Edward expressed his desire to become one of the boys to a new friend and, after a moment of circumspection, was told to come alone to a barn some miles in the country that very night.

The barn was dark and crumbling, and

the door creaked spookily as he pushed it open. Light from candles hung from black-iron holders played on the barn walls, and shadows danced in the corners.

Six human figures sat in a semicircle toward the back of the barn, and all were wearing dark brown hoods, which appeared to have been made out of burlap.

On a small table before them was the old lady's eye. It rested like a jewel on top of a red silken pillow.

Edward approached them fearlessly.

"Welcome," said the one in the middle. "Please be seated."

"But whatever you do," said another, quite ominously, "don't look into the eye!"

My father sat on the ground and waited in silence. He did not look into the eye.

After a moment, the one in the middle spoke again.

"Why are you here?" he asked.

"The eye," Edward said. "I've come for the eye."

"The eye has called you here, has it not?" he said. "Have you not heard the eye calling for you?"

"I have," Edward said. "I have heard the eye call to me."

"Then take the eye and place it in the box, and stay with it all through the night, and re-

turn it here on the morrow. Should anything happen to the eye —"

But the one in the middle stopped
speaking, and there arose a mournful
murmur from the others.

"Should anything happen to eye," he said
again, "if it becomes lost, or broken —"

But here he stopped again, and stared at
my father through the slits in his hood.

"— then we shall take one of your eyes as
recompense," he said.

The six hoods nodded as one.

"I see," my father said, unacquainted with
this rather serious stipulation until now.

"On the morrow, then," he said.

"Yes," said my father. "The morrow."

Leaving the barn and entering into the
dark country night, Edward walked toward
the lights of Auburn, deep in thought. He
didn't know what to do. Would they truly
take one of his own eyes if he failed to return
the glass one tomorrow? Stranger things
have happened. Clutching the box in his
right hand as he walked, he touched his eyes
with his left hand, each of them, and wondered what it would be like if one of them
were gone, and if indeed his vow to the old
lady should be honored when so much was
at stake. He knew it was possible that the

figures in the hoods had no intention of taking one of his eyes, and yet, if there was but a ten percent chance, even a one percent chance that this would happen, was it all worth it? His eyes were real, after all, and the old woman's eye just made of glass. . . .

He stayed up with the eye all night, staring into its shiny blueness, seeing himself within it, until the sun, rising above the tree line the next morning, seemed to him to be the shining eye of some forgotten god.

The barn looked different in the light of day — not so scary. Just an old barn with missing slats, hay poking through holes like stuffing out a pillow. Cows chewing on the grass, an old brown horse fenced in nearby, nose full of air. Edward hesitated at the barn door, then pushed it open, its creakiness not so spooky now.

"You're late," someone said.

Edward looked to the back of the barn but there were no hooded figures this time, just six college boys, roughly as old as Edward was, dressed about the same — loafers, khaki trousers, light blue button-down cotton shirts.

"You're late," he said again, and Edward recognized the voice from the night before. He was the one in the middle, the leader.

Edward looked at him for a long moment.

"Sorry," Edward said. "There was somebody I had to see."

"Do you have the eye?" he asked him.

"Yes," Edward said. "The eye is here."

The man pointed to the small box Edward clutched in his hand.

"Give it here then," he said.

Edward gave the man the box, and as the others crowded around to see, he opened it.

They stared into the box for what seemed a long time, then all of them turned to Edward.

"It's not here," the leader said, almost in a whisper, his face turning red with fury. "The eye's not here!" he screamed.

All at once they came for him, until Edward raised his hand and said, "I told you the eye was here. I didn't say it was in the box."

The six boys stopped, fearing the eye was somewhere on my father's person, and that if they were to beat him badly they might end up hurting the eye as well.

"Give it over!" the leader said. "You have no right! That eye belongs to us."

"Does it?"

It was then the barn door creaked feebly open, and all turned to watch as the old lady, her eye newly restored, came toward them. The six stared, uncomprehending.

"What —" one said, turning to the others. "Who —"

"The eye," my father said. "I told you it was here."

And as the old lady drew near they could see that it was here indeed, not in the box but back in the old lady's head. And though they would have run they couldn't. And though they would have turned away they couldn't, and as she looked at each of them, each of them in turn stared deeply into the old lady's eye, and it was said that within the eye each of them could see their future. And one screamed at what he saw there, and one cried, but one merely looked deeply into the eye uncomprehending, then looked up at my father and stared, as if he knew him now in a different way.

Finally she was done, and all of them ran out the barn door and into the bright morning.

Thus Edward's short stay in Auburn began, and he was rarely ever bothered by anybody, for he was thought to be under the protection of the old lady and her all-seeing eye. He began attending classes and became an A student. He had a good memory. He remembered everything he read, everything he saw. And he remembered the face of the leader in the barn that day, just as the leader would remember Edward's.

It was the face of the man my mother almost married.

My Father's Death: *Take 2*

It happens like this. Old Dr. Bennett, our family doctor, comes out of the guest room and gently shuts the door behind him. Older than old, he looks like the core of an apple left out in the sun. He was there when I was born, and he was old even then. My mother and I are sitting in the living room waiting for his word. Removing the stethoscope from his ears, he looks hopelessly at us.

He says, "There's nothing I can do. I'm sorry. If you have any peace to make with Edward, anything to say at all, now might be . . ." and he trails off into a murmuring silence.

This is something we'd been expecting, this final observation. My mother and I sigh. There's both sadness and relief in the way the tension leaves our bodies, and we look at each other, sharing that look, that once-in-a-lifetime look. I'm a little surprised that the day has finally come, for even though Dr. Bennett had given him a year to live about a year ago, he has been dying so long that in a way I just expect him to keep on dying forever.

"Maybe I should go in first," she says. She looks battered, war-weary, her smile lifeless and somehow serene. "Unless you want to."

"No," I say. "You go and then —"

"If anything —"

"Fine," I say. "Just let me know."

She takes a breath, stands, walks like a somnambulist into his room, leaving the door open behind her. Dr. Bennett, slightly hunched as though his bones have melted in his old age, stands at vacant attention in the middle of the living room, in dark amazement at the powers of life and death. After a few minutes my mother returns, wipes a tear from her cheek, and gives Dr. Bennett a hug. He has known her longer than I have, I think. She is old, too, but next to him she seems forever young. She seems a young woman about to become a widow.

"William," she says.

And so I go in. The room is dim, the grayness of an afternoon nap, though beyond the curtains you can see the outside light bursting to come in. This is the guest room. This is where some of my friends stayed when they used to spend the night, before high school was over and all that, and now it's the room where my father is dying, nearly dead. When I come in he smiles. Dying, he has that look dying people get in

83

their eyes sometimes, happy and sad, tired and spiritually blessed, all at the same time. I've seen it on television. When the main character dies he stays buoyant until the end, dispensing advice to loved ones in his weakening voice, being falsely optimistic about his terminal prognosis, and generally making people cry because he's taking things so well. But it's different with my father. He isn't buoyant or falsely hopeful at all. In fact he's fond of saying, "*Why* am I *still* alive? I *feel* like I should have died a long time ago."

He looks like it, too. His barely over-middle-age body looks as if it has been dug up out of the ground and resuscitated for another go at it, and though he has never had much hair in the first place — he was an old pro at the comb-over — what little hair he did have is gone, and his skin color is a weird shade of true white, so that when I look at him the word that comes to mind is *curdled*.

My dad has curdled.

"You know," he says to me that day. "You know what I'd like?"

"What's that, Dad?"

"A glass of water," he says. "A glass of water would really hit the spot about now."

"Done," I say, and I bring him a glass of

water, which he takes shakily to his lips, dribbling some down his chin, and looking up to me with those eyes as if to say he could have lived a long life — or a longer life, anyway, than he is going to live — without me having to see him dribble water down his chin.

"Sorry," he says.

"Don't worry about it," I say. "You didn't spill that much."

"Not about that," he says, and he shoots me a painful gaze.

"Well, apology accepted," I say. "But you know, you've been a real trooper through this whole thing. Mom and I are real proud of you."

To which he doesn't say anything, because even though he is dying he is still my father, and he doesn't appreciate being spoken to like a schoolboy. In the past year we have switched places; I have become the father, and he the sickly son, whose comportment under these extreme circumstances I value.

"Oh, boy," he says wearily, as if he has been knocked in the head. "What were we just talking about?"

"Water," I say, and he nods, remembering, and takes another sip.

Then he smiles.

"What's so funny?" I say.

"I was just thinking," he says, "that I'll be getting out of this guest room just in time for guests."

He laughs, or does what passes for a laugh these days, what amounts to an exerted wheeze. It had been his decision to move to the guest room some time ago. Although he'd wanted to die at home, with us, he hadn't wanted to die in the bedroom he and Mom had shared for the last few decades, inasmuch as he felt it might ruin things for her in the future. Dying and moving out of the guest room just in time for an out-of-town relative attending his funeral to use it is a witticism he has repeated a dozen times in the last few weeks, each time as if it has just come to him. Which it has, I suppose. He tells it with the same freshness every time and I can't help but smile at the effort.

And so we're stuck here, smiles on our faces like a couple of idiots. What is it you say now, what peace is there to be made in the last minutes of the last day that will mark the before and after of your life until then, the day that will change everything for both of you, the living and the dead? It's three-ten in the afternoon. Outside, it's summer. This morning I'd made plans to go to a movie later in the evening with a friend home from college. My mother is making an eggplant casserole for dinner. She's already laid out the ingredients on the kitchen counter. Before Dr. Bennett came out with his news, I'd decided to go out back and jump in the pool, which, until recently, my father has practically lived in, swimming being the only exercise he was capable of. The swimming pool is right outside the guest room window. Mother thinks my swimming keeps him awake sometimes, but he likes to hear me swimming. The splashing, he says, makes him feel a little wet himself.

Slowly we lose our idiot smiles and just look at each other, plainly.

"Hey," my father says. "I'll miss you."

"And me you."

"Really?" he says.

"Of course, Dad. I'm the one —"

"Still here," he says. "So it figures that you'd be the one doing the missing."

"Do you," I say, as if the words are being willed by a force inside of me, "do you believe —"

I stop myself. There's an unspoken rule in my family that it's best not to talk religion or politics with my father. When the subject is religion he won't talk at all, and when it's politics he won't stop talking. The truth is, most things are hard to talk about with him.

By that I mean the *essence* of things, the important things, the things that matter. Somehow it's just too hard for him, and maybe a bit dicey, a chore for this very intelligent man who has forgotten more facts about geography and math and history than I've ever learned (he knew the capitals of all fifty states, and where you'd end up if you flew due east from New York). So I edit my thoughts as much as I can. But sometimes a few indelicate words escape.

"Believe what?" he asks me, fixing me with those eyes, those small blue eyes, trapping me there. So I say it.

"In Heaven," I say.

"Do I believe in Heaven?"

"And God and all that stuff," I say, because I don't know. I don't know if he believes in God or life after death or the possibility that we all come back as someone or something else. I don't know if he believes in Hell, either, or angels, or the Elysian Fields, or the Loch Ness Monster. We never talked about these things when he was healthy, and since he's gotten sick all we've talked about is medication and the sports teams he can no longer follow because he falls asleep the second someone turns the TV on, and ways of getting through the pain. And I expect him to ignore it now. But suddenly his eyes widen and seem to clear, as if he were seized by the prospect of what awaited him after his death — other than an empty guest room. As if this is the first time the thought has occurred to him.

"What a question," he says, his voice rising full. "I don't know if I can really say, one way or the other. But that reminds me — and stop me if you've heard this one — of the day Jesus was watching the gates for St. Peter. Anyway, Jesus is giving him a hand one day when a man walks shuffling up the path to Heaven.

" 'What have you done to enter the kingdom of Heaven?' Jesus asks him.

"And the man says, 'Well, not much really. I'm just a poor carpenter who led a quiet life. The only remarkable thing about my life was my son.'

" 'Your son?' Jesus asks, getting interested.

" 'Yes, he was a quite a son,' the man says. 'He went through a most unusual birth and later a great transformation. He also became quite well known throughout the world and is still loved by many today.'

"Christ looks at the man, embraces him tightly, and says 'Father, father!'

"And the old man hugs him back and says, 'Pinocchio?' "

He wheezes, I smile, shaking my head.

"Heard it," I say.

"You were supposed to stop me," he says, clearly exhausted after the telling. "How many *breaths* do I have left? You don't want me to waste them on twice-told jokes, do you?"

"It's not like you've learned any new ones lately," I say. "Anyway, this is sort of a best-of thing. A compilation. Edward Bloom's Collected Jokes. They're funny, Dad, don't worry. But you didn't answer my question."

"What question?"

I don't know whether to laugh or cry. He's lived his whole life like a turtle, within an emotional carapace that makes for the perfect defense: there's absolutely no way in. My hope is that in these last moments he'll show me the vulnerable and tender underbelly of his self, but this isn't happening, yet, and I'm a fool to think that it will. This is the way it has gone from the beginning: every time we get close to something meaningful, serious, or delicate, he tells a joke. There is never a yes or no, what do *you* think, here, according to me, is the meaning of life.

"Why do you think that is?" I say out loud, as though he can hear me thinking.

And somehow, he can.

"Never felt comfortable addressing these

things head-on," he says, moving uncomfortably beneath his sheets. "Who really knows for certain? Proof is unavailable. So one day I think yes, the next no. Other days, I'm on the fence. Is there a God? Some days I really believe there is, others, I'm not so sure. Under these less than ideal conditions, a good joke somehow seems more appropriate. At least you can laugh."

"But a joke," I say. "It's funny for a minute or two and that's it. You're left with nothing. Even if you changed your mind every other day I'd rather — I wished you'd shared some of these things with me. Even your doubts would have been better than a constant stream of jokes."

"You're right," he says, leaning back hard into his pillow and looking toward the ceiling, as though he can't believe that I have chosen now, of all times, to give him this assignment. It's a burden, and I see it weighing on him, pressing the life right out, and I truly can't believe I did it, said it the way I have.

"Still," he says, "if I shared my doubts with you, about God and love and life and death, that's all you'd have: a bunch of doubts. But now, see, you've got all these great jokes."

"They're not all so great," I say.

The central air hums on, billowing the shades open at the bottom. Light streams in past the blinds, dust motes swimming. The room has a faint stench to it, which I thought I'd gotten used to, but haven't. It always makes me sick to my stomach and I feel it coming on strong now. It's either that or the shock to my system of having learned more about my father in the last few seconds than I have in the lifetime that preceded them.

His eyes close and I'm scared, my heart jumps, and I feel as though I should get Mother, but as I begin to move away he grips my hand lightly in his own.

"I was a good dad," he says.

A statement of not unassailable fact he leaves hanging there, as if for my appraisal. I look at him, at it.

"You *are* a good dad," I say.

"Thanks," he says, and his eyelids flutter a bit, as if he's heard what he's come to hear. This is what is meant by last words: they are keys to unlock the afterlife. They're not last words but passwords, and as soon as they're spoken you can go.

"So. What is it today, Dad?"

"What is what?" he says dreamily.

"God and Heaven and all that. What do you think: yes or no? Maybe tomorrow you'll feel differently, I understand that. But now, right now, what are you feeling? I really want to know, Dad. Dad?" I say, for he seems to be drifting away from me into the deepest sleep. *"Dad?"* I say.

And he opens his eyes and looks at me with his pale baby blues suddenly full of an urgency and he says, he says to me, he says to his son sitting beside his bed waiting for him to die, he says, *"Pinocchio?"*

His First Great Love

It was my father's great joy and misfortune to fall in love with the most beautiful woman in the town of Auburn, and possibly in the entire state of Alabama, Miss Sandra Kay Templeton.

Why misfortune? Because he was not the only man in Auburn, and possibly not the only man in the rest of the entire state of Alabama, to be in love with her. He took a number and headed to the end of the line.

Her beauty had already been celebrated in song by one talented admirer:

> Sandy, Sandy, Sandy
> You're a pretty girl
> Hop into my car
> And I'll take you for a whirl . . .

And so on.

There had also been duels, car races, drinking bouts, bare-fisted fights dedicated to her affection, and there was at least one dog named after her, and there might have been more.

Sandra didn't intend to be as beautiful as

she was. It wasn't her desire to be loved by so many men — one would do fine. But she couldn't help being pretty, or the kind of pretty that was so widely admired, and as soon as she discouraged one suitor another popped up to take his place, with flowers, songs, ready to fight. So she just minded her own business, and let everybody else mind theirs, and a line formed behind her, a veritable club, a kind of fraternity of wishful thinking and broken hearts.

Edward didn't write any songs. For a long time he didn't do anything. He looked at her, of course. He didn't mind looking at her when she passed; looking brought its own special excitement with it. It was as if she brought her own light with her, because wherever she went, she glowed. Who could explain that?

Edward liked to catch that glow once in a while.

His Legendary Legs

He was so fast it was said he could arrive in a place before setting out to get there. It was not running so much as it was flight, his legs seeming never to touch the ground but move across a current of air. He never asked to race but many asked to race him, and though he tried to dissuade them, a young man's taunts and jibes are not easily sustained. He would end up, invariably, removing his shoes — for he never ran in his shoes — and waiting for his eager counterpart to get ready. Then they were off — or rather, it was over, for there was never any race to speak of. Before the young man who wished so to test his skills against those of my father had even left the starting line, he viewed at the finish the dim figure of the man he had hoped to beat.

In Which He Makes His Move

To make a long story not quite so long, well, pretty soon it wasn't enough for him just to see her anymore. He had to get close to her, he had to talk, he had to touch.

He followed her around for a while. He followed her between classes, down the halls, this sort of thing. Brushed against her accidentally. Touched her arm in the cafeteria.

"Excuse me," he always said.

She got into his brain and drove him crazy. One day he watched her sharpening a pencil. Her soft hands holding the long yellow shaft. He picked up the shavings that fell on the floor and rubbed them between his thumb and forefinger. Then one day he saw her talking to someone he thought he knew. She was smiling in a way he'd never seen her smile before. He watched them talk and laugh for a few minutes, and then his heart fell as he watched her look around, then slowly lean in for a kiss. He almost decided not to pursue her when he saw this, but then he placed the face. It was the guy from the barn, the one who had stolen the old lady's eye. His name was Don Price.

97

My father's feeling was that if he had defeated him once, he could do it again.

His chance came on the following day. His whole body was about to explode from desire. The blood was tight against his skin. Somehow he needed to release the pressure. He saw Sandra in the hallway.

"Sandra," he said, picking an inopportune moment — she was just entering the ladies' room. "You don't know me. You probably have never even seen me before. But I was wondering — if this is something you would consider, I mean — well, that this Friday night maybe we could go out somewhere together. If you want."

Not surprisingly, at that precise moment she was feeling the same way he was: her body was about to explode, the blood was tight against her skin, and she needed to release the pressure.

"Well, yes," she said, without seeming to think much about it. "Friday would be nice," and just that quickly she disappeared into the ladies' room.

Yes, she said, even though just that morning Don Price had asked her to marry him. She'd almost said yes to that, too, but then something had told her to take a few days to think about it, as though my father had sent his hope on a whisper, and she had heard it.

The Fight

Edward Bloom was not a fighter. He enjoyed the pleasures of human discourse too much to resort to such a primitive and often painful form of settling disputes. But he could defend himself when forced to, and he was forced to the night he took Sandra Kay Templeton for a drive down the road on Piney Mountain.

Three weeks had passed since their first date, and between then and now many words had passed between Edward and Sandra. They'd gone to a movie together, split a couple of malts, he'd even told her a joke or two. Simply by being who he was — no more, no less — my father was winning my mother's heart. Things were getting serious: when he touched her hand, she blushed. She'd forget the end of sentences she'd begun. It wasn't that she'd fallen in love with my father, yet. But she saw that she *could*.

Maybe she had a lot more thinking to do.

This night would be an important part of the whole thinking process. It was the night of The Drive. After a few miles of driving aimlessly they'd find themselves at the end of some country dead-end road, alone in the dark woods, and as the silence surrounded them he would lean toward her and she'd move imperceptibly toward him and they would fall into a kiss. And they were heading that way when in the rearview mirror my father saw a pair of headlights, small at first but getting larger, heading fast down the thin and twisting road on Piney Mountain. Edward didn't know it was Don Price. He only knew it was a car coming up behind them at a dangerous speed, and so he slowed down, the better to make a wise decision if something was to happen.

Suddenly the car was directly behind them, its headlights glaring in the rearview mirror. Edward rolled down his window and motioned the car by, but when he did so it bumped his fender. Sandra gasped, and my father touched her leg with his hand to calm her.

"It's okay," he said. "Probably some drunk kid."

"No," she said. "That's Don."

And my father understood. Without another word, the situation was clear, just as it would have been one hundred years before in a frontier town out west and Don had met him in the middle of a dusty street, hand on his holster. This was a showdown.

Don's car bumped the fender again, and my father hit the gas. Edward had to prove that if fast was what Don Price wanted, Edward could be fast, and being fast he sped around the next curve, leaving Don Price in the distance behind him.

He was back, though, in just seconds, no longer bumping from behind but side by side now, the two cars taking up the entire road, speeding over hills and turns that would have led weaker hearts to stop, then and there. Don Price edged his car into my father's lane, and my father edged back, the two cars scraping door to door. My father knew he could drive this road as long as he needed to, but he wasn't sure about Don Price, whose face he caught a glimpse of as their cars veered back and forth, reeling from the jouncing. The boy had been drinking, for sure.

My father gave the car one last shot of acceleration, pulled ahead, and turned the wheel abruptly, blocking the road with his car. Don Price braked just feet away, and both men were out of their cars in an instant, eye to eye and only an arm's length away.

"She's mine," Don Price said.

He was as big as Edward, even bigger

around the shoulders. His father owned a trucking company, where Don worked summers loading and unloading tractor trailers, and it showed.

"I didn't know that she belonged to anybody," my father said.

"Well, now you do, farm boy," Don said.

Don looked at her, still sitting in the car.

"Sandra," he said.

But she didn't move. She just sat there, thinking.

"We're getting married," Don said to my father. "I've asked her to marry me, farm boy. Or didn't she tell you?"

"The question is, what did she tell you?"

Don Price didn't say anything, but his breathing came faster and his eyes narrowed, like a bull about to charge.

"I could tear you apart like a paper doll," he said.

"There's no reason for that," my father said.

"You better hope there's not," Don Price said. "As long as Sandy gets in my car. Now."

"She's not going to be doing that, Don," my father said.

Don Price laughed.

"Who the hell are you to say?"

"You're drunk, Don," he said. "I'll drive

her down off the mountain, and then if she wants to go with you she can. How about that?"

But this just made Don Price laugh even harder. Even though he remembered what he had seen in the glass of the old lady's eye many weeks ago, Don Price just laughed.

"Thanks for giving me a goddamn choice, farm boy," he said. "But no thanks."

And Don Price came at my father with the fury of ten men, but my father had the strength of many more, and they fought for some time, beating each other with their fists. Blood covered both their faces, streaming from their noses and lips, but in the end Don Price fell and did not get up, and my father stood over him, triumphant. Then he placed his opponent's limp and aching body into the back seat of his car, and drove Don Price and my mother off the mountain and back into town. He drove until they arrived at my mother's dorm, and parked in the darkness of the late night, with Don Price still moaning softly in the back.

Neither my mother nor my father spoke for a long time. It was a silence so still one could almost hear the other's thoughts. Then my father said, "He asked you to marry him, Sandy?"

"Yes," my mother said. "He did."

"And so what did you tell him?" he asked her.

"I told him that I'd think about it," she said.

"And?" my father said.

"And I've thought about it," she said, taking my father's bloody hand in her own.

They fell into a kiss.

On Meeting the In-Laws

According to my father, my mother's father had no hair anywhere on his body. He owned a farm in the country, where he lived with his wife, bedridden by then for ten years, unable to feed herself or talk, and he rode a great horse, as big as any horse there was, and black, with a spot of white on each of its legs just above the hooves.

He adored my mother. He had told amazing stories about her since she was little, and now that he was old and had lost some of his mind it appeared that he had begun to believe them.

He thought she hung the moon. He actually believed this from time to time. He believed the moon wouldn't have been there but that she'd hung it. He believed the stars were wishes, and that one day they would all come true. For her, his daughter. He had told her this when she was little to make her happy, and now that he was old he believed it, because it made him happy and because he was so very old.

He had not been invited to the wedding. How this could happen is simple: no one had. It was not a wedding as much as it was a legal proceeding at the Auburn courthouse, with strangers as witnesses and a febrile old judge as minister, pronouncing in his drawl, with little bits of white spittle gathering in the corners of his mouth, that from this moment forward you are now man and wife till death do you part et cetera. And thus it was done.

This wasn't going to be easy to explain to Mr. Templeton, but my father wanted to give it a try. He drove up to the gate of the farm, where there was a sign that read STOP BLOW HORN and by coincidence there, too, was his new wife's father, atop his horse, much bigger than life, suspiciously eyeing the long car, from which his daughter shyly waved. He opened the gate by slipping a piece of wood from a six-inch-wide slit carved into a fence post, and my father drove slowly, so as not to spook the horse.

He drove on up to the house, Mr. Templeton following on horseback. My mother and father were quiet. He looked over at her and smiled.

"There's nothing to worry about," he said.

"Who's worried?" she said, laughing.

Though neither of them seemed particularly reassured.

★ ★ ★

"Daddy," she said up at the house, "I want you to meet Edward Bloom. Edward, Seth Templeton. Now y'all shake hands."

They did.

Mr. Templeton looked at his daughter.

"Why am I doing this?" he said.

"Doing what?"

"Shaking this man's hand?"

" 'Cause he's my husband," she said. "We got married, Daddy."

He kept shaking, looking deep into Edward's eyes. Then he laughed. It sounded like the burst from a firecracker.

"Married!" he said, and he walked inside. The newlyweds followed. He brought them a couple of Cokes from the icebox, and they sat down in the living room, where Mr. Templeton stuffed an ivory-stemmed pipe full of black tobacco and lit it, and the room was suddenly overcast with a thin layer of smoke, which hung just above their heads.

"So what's all this about?" he said, sucking away and coughing.

It was a question that seemed difficult to answer, so neither of them said anything. They just smiled. Edward stared at the man's hairless, egglike head, then into his eyes.

"I love your daughter, Mr. Templeton,"

my father said. "And I'm going to love her and take care of her for the rest of my life."

My father had thought of what he was going to say for a long time, and he'd come up with these simple, yet profound, words. He thought they said everything that needed saying, and hoped Mr. Templeton would think so, too.

"Bloom, you say?" Mr. Templeton said, squinting. "Knew a man named Bloom once. Rode with him. 1918, 1919, I was in the cavalry. Stationed in Yellowstone. In those days there were bandits. You may not have realized that. Mexican bandits mostly. Horse thieves and just regular thieves. We chased our share of them, Bloom and me. Along with the others, of course. Rogerson, Mayberry, Stimson. Right into Mexico. Oh yes. Our share. We chased them. Right into Mexico, Mr. Bloom. Right into Mexico."

My father nodded, smiled, sipped on his Coke. Mr. Templeton hadn't heard a word he said.

"You have a nice-looking horse out there," my father said.

"You know about horses, then?" he said, and laughed again — popping, gravelly sounds. "You've found a man who knows something about horses, haven't you, dear?"

"I think I have, Daddy," she said.

"That's good," he said, nodding. "That's very good."

The day passed in just this way. Mr. Templeton told stories of his days in the cavalry, and laughed, and the conversation turned to religion and Jesus, a favorite topic of Mr. Templeton's, for it was his belief that the crucifixion was an especially dastardly act, seeing as how Pontius Pilate and Jesus had been roommates at Oxford. In this light Pontius Pilate had really done the Lord dirty. No more mention was made of the marriage the rest of that afternoon — Mr. Templeton, in fact, seemed to forget why they were there at all — and as dusk came on it was time to leave.

The three of them stood, the men shook hands again, and they walked past the closed bedroom door and slowed there. Sandra looked at her father, who shook his head.

"Not a good day," he said. "Best not disturb her."

And so they left, the two of them, waving at the old man through the darkening light, and him waving back at them and pointing, with a child's delight, toward the starry sky.

His Three Labors

Because it was a great metropolis full of hope, my parents moved to Birmingham, Alabama, where my father sought his fortune. Word of his great strength, intelligence, and perseverance had spread even this far, and yet his youth was such that my father knew he must perform many great labors before he assumed his rightful place.

His first labor was to work as a veterinarian's assistant. As a veterinarian's assistant, his most important responsibility was to clean out the dog kennels and cat cages. Every morning when he arrived, the cages and kennels would be nearly filled with feces. Some of it would lie on the paper he'd placed down the night before, but still more would be smeared on the walls, and some of it on the very animals themselves. My father cleaned this mess up every morning and every evening. He did it until the cages shone, until you could have eaten a meal off the surface of the floor, so spotless and clean had he left it. But it would only take a few seconds for it to get soiled again, and this was the job's terrible Sisyphean frustration:

a dog might look straight at you, just as you were locking him into his lovely, newly cleaned cage, and shit.

His second labor was as a sales clerk in the lingerie section of a department store downtown, called Smith's. The fact that he had been stationed in lingerie seemed a cruel joke, and indeed, he suffered greatly from the sassy comments he heard from the men in other departments — especially from the men in sportswear. But he persevered, and eventually won the trust of the women who regularly shopped at Smith's, and in fact came to be preferred to the women who worked with him. They valued his keen eye.

But there was one woman who was never able to accept my father as a sales clerk. Her name was Muriel Rainwater. She had lived in Birmingham all her life, had two husbands, both dead, no children at all, and money beyond counting to get through before she passed on herself. She was almost eighty years old then, and, much like a tree, each year had seen her girth expand until she'd become monumental; still, she was quite vain. While she didn't care to be much thinner than she was, she certainly wanted to look much thinner, and thus often visited the lingerie department at Smith's searching for the latest in girdles.

And so every month Mrs. Rainwater marched down to Smith's and sat down in one of the large, overstuffed chairs provided for its customers, and, without a word, merely nodded toward a clerk, and that clerk duly brought her the latest in girdle wear. But that clerk was never Edward Bloom.

This was clearly a snub. But the truth was that Edward was not particularly fond of Mrs. Rainwater, either. No one was — the way her feet smelled of moth balls, her hair like burnt fabric, and the way her arms shook when she pointed at something she wanted. But the fact that she insisted on not allowing him to serve her made her, to Edward, the most desirable customer in the store. He made it his goal to one day wait on Muriel Rainwater.

To this end he pirated the next shipment of girdles and hid them in a corner of the warehouse, where only he could find them. Mrs. Rainwater came in the very next day. She sat down in an overstuffed chair and pointed at one of the girls.

"You!" she said. "Bring me the girdle!"

The girl grew flustered, for she feared Mrs. Rainwater.

"The girdle?" she said. "But none have arrived!"

"Oh yes they have!" Mrs. Rainwater said, her mouth wide and gaping like a cave. "I know they have arrived! You!" she said, pointing to another, her arm sloshing like a water balloon. "If she can't serve me, you can. Bring me the girdle!"

This girl ran crying from the floor. The next girl fell to her knees before Mrs. Rainwater even said a word.

Finally, no one was left to point at but my father. He stood at the far end of the showroom floor, tall and proud. She saw him, but pretended not to. She pretended he wasn't there at all.

"Can someone please help me?" she screamed. "I want to see the new girdle! Can someone please —"

My father crossed the showroom floor and stood before her.

"What do you want?" she said.

"Here to serve you, Mrs. Rainwater."

Mrs. Rainwater shook her head and stared at her feet; she looked like she wanted to spit.

"Men don't belong in this department!" she cried.

"And yet," he said, "here I am. And I alone know where the new girdles are. I alone can help you."

"No!" she said, shaking her head in disbelief, her big horse eyes plainly shocked. "This can't be . . . I, I —"

"I'd be happy to get it for you, Mrs. Rainwater. More than happy."

"Fine then!" she said, little bits of spittle collecting at the corners of her mouth. "Get me the girdle!"

And so he did. Mrs. Rainwater stood. She waddled to the changing room, where the girdle rested on a stool. She slammed the door behind her. My father heard her grunt and groan and snap and tighten and finally, some minutes later, she emerged.

And she was no longer Mrs. Rainwater. She had been completely transformed. The girdle had taken her, this whale of a woman, and turned her into beauty itself. She did have a bounteous breast, and a rear end of some proportion, but her figure was all wavy and smooth rolls, and she even seemed younger, and sweeter, and certainly a happier woman than before. It was indeed a technological miracle.

She looked at my father as though he were a god.

"This is it!" she cried, her voice a melodious tune. "This is the girdle I've been waiting for all my life! And to think that you — you — I've been so unfair! Can you ever forgive me?"

Then she turned from him and faced a mirror, where she enthusiastically admired her new self.

"Oh, yes," she said. "Oh my, yes. This is how I was meant to look. With this, I can probably get a new husband. I never thought girdles could come so far so quickly! But look at me! Just look!"

She turned and gave my father an adoring glance.

"You'll go far here, young man," she said.

The third and last labor Edward Bloom performed had to do with a wild dog. After being speedily promoted from sales clerk to manager, my mother and father moved into a small white house across the street from the elementary school. They were only the second family to live in that house. It had been built by Amos Calloway, sixty years before, and he and his wife had raised a family there, and the children had all moved away. Mrs. Calloway had died many years before, and when Mr. Calloway died, everyone in the neighborhood assumed one of their lovely children would move back there to live. But they didn't. The children had their own lives rooted in distant towns and cities, and, after burying their father, promptly put the house on the market, which the Blooms felt lucky to have snatched up.

But the Blooms weren't welcome — not in Amos Calloway's house. Amos Calloway's association with the house he built was so strong that following his death, some in the neighborhood suggested that the structure be razed and a park built for the children there. Now that the Calloways had departed, maybe the house should go, too. For some strange new couple to come in and live there was like — it was like two people trying to squeeze into Amos Calloway's coffin, his own body just freshly placed there. In short, nobody much liked the Blooms.

My mother and father did what they could to change this. My mother took in stray cats, just as she learned Mrs. Calloway had done. My father continued to trim the frontage azaleas into the shapes of the alphabet, something Amos was locally famous for. All for nothing. On weekends my mother and father worked out in the yard, just as their neighbors did, but it was as if they were invisible. And in a way, they were. In order to bear the absence of Amos Calloway and his family, the neighborhood had chosen to disregard the Blooms' presence.

Until there came a day when the neighborhood was invaded by a pack of wild dogs. Who knows where they came from. Six, eight, some say ten — they tore through the trash cans at night, and dug deep holes in the gardens. The velvety canvas of sleep was torn by their terrible howls and vicious snarls. Other dogs who dared to face them were found dead the next morning, or never found at all. Children were not allowed outside past dusk, and some of the men took to carrying guns with them everywhere they went. Finally, the town called in officials from the State Bureau of Animal Control, and on one bloody night all the wild dogs were either killed or captured.

All but one, that is. And he was the fiercest, most terrible dog of all. Pitch black, he blended with the night. It was said he was so stealthy you wouldn't know he was even near you — until he showed you his bright shining teeth. And this dog was not merely wild: he was a crazed, lunatic dog, with a seeming human capacity for rage and retribution. One family paid dearly when they installed an electric fence around their property. Watching out the window one night they saw the dog walk into it. He was shocked and thrown back into the street, but essentially unharmed. After that the dog toured the edge of this family's property almost exclusively, with the effect that, through the night at least, no one came in and no went out. It was as though, instead of protection, the family had built a prison for themselves.

At any time in his life, my father could have tamed the dog and led him back into the hills from whence he came; such was his way with animals. And yet he didn't. Why? Because for once, he couldn't. The rigors of his new life had weakened him. It wasn't a reluctance to use the strengths and powers he was born with; he simply didn't seem to possess them anymore.

And the marauding would have continued if Fate hadn't nudged my father in the small of his back, urging him to leave the house one night and take a walk. The streets of Edgewood were empty, of course: who dared brave these streets after the sun had gone down, knowing, as they did, that the Helldog (as he'd come to be known) was out there, somewhere? My father thought little of the dog, however; he wasn't the kind of man who structured his life around a canine peril. Or perhaps my father was the agent of some greater power. All we know for certain is this: he went for a walk one night and saved a child's life.

The child — three-year-old Jennifer Morgan, who lived just two doors down from the old Calloway place, as it was still called — had wandered out the kitchen door while her parents were working to unclog a toilet in the master bedroom. She'd heard so much about the dog outside that she could no longer resist: she had to go out and pet him. When my father saw her, she was walking toward the feral black presence with a piece of bread in her hand, calling, "Here doggy. Doggy, come here."

The Helldog was coming at a leisurely gait, unable to believe his luck. He had never eaten a little girl before, but he'd heard they were tasty. Better than little boys, anyway, and almost as good as chickens.

The culinary ecstasy of the moment was interrupted, however, by Edward Bloom. He scooped the girl up in his arms and tossed the bread to the dog, who ignored it and kept coming. At any other time his fabled power with the animals would have beguiled the dog into docility. However, the big black Helldog was aggravated. Edward had rudely come between him and a meal.

The dog came at them in a fury and jumped. Holding the girl in one arm, Bloom reached out with the other and grabbed the dog by his neck, then slammed him to the ground. The dog yelped, but got back on all fours and growled with a frightful seriousness. His head swung from side to side with a dizzying speed; for a moment he looked as if he had two heads, growling and baring two sets of teeth and pink-white gums.

By this time, the Morgans had noticed their little girl was missing and had come running in the direction of the dog's terrible howl. They arrived in time to see the dog lunge once more, this time barely missing my father's neck, his warm moist breath spraying past. This was the dog's fatal mistake: leaving his bare underside exposed as he jumped so high into the air, Edward Bloom was able to thrust his hand through the dog's hair and skin and into the body proper, clutching and finally ripping out his massive beating heart. My father held the girl so close, nestled into his wide shoulder, that she was spared this last gory scene. As the dog fell heavy to the ground my father dropped the heart there also, and handed the girl to her parents, and continued his walk into the night.

Thus ended the three labors of Edward Bloom.

He Goes to War

He wasn't a general, or a captain, or an officer of any kind. He wasn't the medic, he wasn't the poet, he wasn't the cynic, he wasn't the lover, and he wasn't the radio operator. He was, of course, a sailor. Across the foamy sea he rolled with hundreds of others, aboard an invulnerable vessel called the *Neried*. This was a ship as big as his hometown — bigger, even. Certainly, there were more people aboard the *Neried* than lived within the city limits of Ashland, though he had put a great distance between himself and that town. Since leaving, he had accomplished many great things, and now he was accomplishing the greatest of all: defending the free world. He felt, in an odd way, that the world rested on his shoulders. That, even though he was merely a sailor, without even a medal, without decoration of any kind, somehow the entire effort hinged on his ability to see it through. It was good to be a part of this crew, then, on this invulnerable ship, slipping through the wine-dark sea. Being surrounded by water, by horizons everywhere he looked, made him consider the greater world lying beyond, and the possibility that the world held out to him. Being surrounded by water made him feel secure and at peace.

This is how he was feeling when a torpedo ripped into the hull. The ship felt like it had run aground, and Edward was thrown four feet across the deck. The ship began to list.

"All hands on deck!" the loudspeaker boomed. "Blow up your life belts!"

My father, a part of him in shock, thinking *This isn't supposed to happen,* found his life belt and tied one of the cords around his neck and the other around his waist. He looked around him, annoyed, *This isn't supposed to happen,* but far from panic. No one around him panicked, either. Everyone was amazingly cool, as if this were a drill. But the *Neried* was listing to port.

The captain's voice came through then on the loudspeaker.

"All hands on deck. Prepare to abandon ship."

Still there was no alarm, no hurry. Those on the flag deck moved toward a companionway leading to the quarterdeck. There was no pushing. Edward smiled at his friends, and they smiled back, even though the ship they were on was going down.

On deck he saw the extent of his new reality. Men were tossing rafts overboard as well as pieces of wood, life belts, benches, anything that would float. Then they jumped into sea after them. But the ship was like a series of ledges. Many misjudged the distance, hit the side of the ship, and slid into the sea. Everywhere men were flinging themselves into the water. Hundreds of heads, like human buoys, were bobbing in the water. The propeller was still turning, and some of the men were sucked into its turning blades. Edward sat down on the edge of the ship and removed the last letter he had received from his wife. "Not a day goes by that I don't think of you. I even pray — just started. Feels good. Hope it helps some." He smiled, refolded the letter, and placed it back in his pocket. He took off his shoes and his socks, and he rolled each sock up in a ball and placed them in the toes of his shoes. He watched as a man near him jumped off the ship and onto another man, and both disappeared. *I don't want to jump on anybody,* he thought, and looked for an open spot. But down below the sea was covered in a sheet of oil, and he didn't want to jump into that, either. So he looked until he found a clear circle of water, a place the oil had yet to saturate, and he pretended to believe he could jump from the side of the ship straight into it.

Miraculously, he did. He jumped the twenty feet from the side of the ship directly into that spot of sea, where he sank fast, and didn't rise. He remained suspended thirty, maybe even forty feet below the surface, like a fly in amber. He could see the ship sinking to one side, and above him hundreds and hundreds of legs of his fellow sailors, like a great giant centipede swimming in the sea. He felt as though he should be drowning by then, but he wasn't. In fact, he seemed to be breathing. Not through his mouth but through his own body. He didn't understand it but he was breathing, and he thought this meant he was dead.

But then, in the distance away from the ship, he saw a young girl waving to him. The same girl, he remembered, from a long time ago, he knew that in a minute. She was waving him toward her, smiling, as though she'd been waiting on him there for some time. He began to swim toward her. Same girl all right. A little older now, as he was. But the same girl. As he got closer she swam out farther, and kept waving. He didn't know how long he was under water like that, swimming toward her, but it was longer than it should have been. He swam until a shaft of sunlight broke through the oil-shrouded sea and he looked up to see there was no oil there, just pure blue. And then he looked for the girl — *young lady,* he corrected himself — but she was gone, too. And all of a sudden he was in need of a breath of fresh air. So he moved toward the surface sunlight, suddenly as light and fast as a bubble himself, and when he popped into the bright world saw how far away he was from everyone. They were treading water, moving slowly through the oil. But they saw Edward waving to them as the girl had waved to him, and it gave them a sense of purpose, even hope, and those who saw him began to swim toward my father as fast as they possibly could. Hundreds of men moved sluggishly through the oil toward him. Some didn't, though. Even some who saw him didn't move. And these were the men who were sucked back under when the *Neried* finally went down. Even as far out as Edward was, he felt the futile tug of the ship on his body, pulling him back. But he wasn't going back. He was going home.

My Father's Death: Take 3

It happens like this. Old Dr. Bennett, our family doctor, comes out of the guest room and gently shuts the door behind him. Older than old, Dr. Bennett has been part of our lives forever, he was even there when I was born, at which time he had been asked by the local medical board to please retire, soon — that's how old he is. Dr. Bennett is now too old for almost anything. He doesn't walk so much as shuffle, doesn't breath so much as gasp. And he seems unable to deal with the consequences of his patient's terminal condition. As he comes out of the guest room, where my father's been staying the last few weeks, Dr. Bennett breaks down in a storm of tears, and for some time can't speak he's crying so much, shoulders heaving, his crumpled old hands cupped over his eyes.

Finally, he's able to look up and gasp for breath. He looks like a lost child, and he says to my mother and me, we who are now prepared for the very worst, "I don't . . . I don't really know what's going on. I can't tell anymore. He seems pretty bad off, though. Best go see for yourself."

My mother looks at me, and it is that look of final resignation I see in her eyes, that look that says she is ready for whatever awaits her beyond the door, however sad or horrible. She is ready. She takes my hand and holds it tight before standing and going in. Dr. Bennett falls into my father's chair and slumps there as if emptied of the will to go on. For a moment I think he's dead. For a moment I think Death has come and passed my father over, and decided to take this one instead. But no. Death has come for my father. Dr. Bennett opens his eyes and stares into the wild, distant empty space before him, and I can guess what he's thinking. *Edward Bloom! Who would have thought! Man of the world! Importer/exporter! We all thought you'd live forever. Though the rest of us fall like leaves from a tree, if there was one to withstand the harsh winter ahead and hang on for dear life we thought it would be you.* As though he were a god. This is how we have come to think of my father. Although we have seen him early in the morning in his boxer shorts, and late at night asleep in front of the television after everything on it has gone off the air, mouth open, blue light like a shroud over his dreaming face, we believe he is somehow divine, a god, the god of laughter, the god who cannot speak but to say, *There was this man*

. . . Or perhaps part god, the product of a mortal woman and some glorious entity descended here to make the world the kind of place where more people laughed, and, inspired by their laughter, bought things from my father to make their lives better, and his life better, and in that way, all lives were made better. He is funny and he makes money and what could be better than that? He even laughs at death, he laughs at my tears. I hear him laughing now, as my mother leaves the room shaking her head.

"Incorrigible," she says. "Completely and totally incorrigible."

She's crying, too, but these are not tears of grief or sadness, those tears have already been shed. These are tears of frustration, of being alive and alone while my father lies in the guest room dying and not dying *right*. I look at her and with my eyes ask, *Should I?* And she shrugs her shoulders as if to say, *It's up to you, go in if you'd like,* and seems to be on the verge of a kind of laughter herself, if she weren't already crying, which is a confusing sort of expression for a face to have to bear.

Dr. Bennett seems to have fallen asleep in my father's chair.

I stand and go to the half-closed door and peer beyond it. My father is sitting up, braced by a load of pillows, still and staring at nothing as though he were on Pause, waiting for someone or something to activate him. Which is what my presence does. When he sees me, he smiles.

"Come in, William," he says.

"Well, you seem to be feeling better," I say, sitting down in the chair beside his bed, the chair I've been sitting in every day for the last few weeks. In my father's journey to the end of his life, this chair is the place I watch from.

"I am feeling better," he says, nodding, taking a deep breath as if to prove it. "I think I am."

But only today, for this moment on this day. There is no turning back now for my father. To get better now would take more than a miracle; it would take a written excuse from Zeus himself, signed in triplicate and sent to every other deity who might lay claim to my father's withered body and soul.

He is already a little bit dead, I think, if such a thing were possible; the metamorphosis that has occurred would be too much to believe if I hadn't seen it myself. At first, small lesions appeared on his arms and legs. They were treated, but to no real effect. Then they appeared to heal on their own eventually — not, however, in a way we might have hoped for or expected. Instead of his soft, white skin with the long black hairs growing out of it like corn silk, his skin has become hard and shiny — indeed, almost scaly, like a second skin. Looking at him isn't hard until you leave the room and see the photo sitting on the fireplace mantel. It was taken six or seven years ago on a beach in California, and when you look at it you can see — a man. He's not a man in the same way now. He's something else altogether.

"Not good, really," he says, revising himself. "I wouldn't say *good*. But better."

"I just wondered what bothered Dr. Bennett," I say. "He seemed really concerned when he came out of here."

My father nods.

"Honestly," he says, in a confidential tone, "I think it was my jokes."

"Your jokes?"

"My doctor jokes. I think he'd heard one too many," and my father begins to recite his litany of tired old jokes:

Doctor, doctor! I've only got 59 seconds to live. Hang on, I'll be with you in a minute.

Doctor, doctor! I keep thinking I'm a pair of curtains. Come on, pull yourself together.

Doctor, doctor! My sister thinks she's in a lift.

130

Tell her to come in. *I can't. She doesn't stop at this floor.*

Doctor, doctor! I feel like a goat. Stop acting like a little kid.

Doctor, doctor! I think I'm shrinking. You'll just have to be a little patient.

"I know a million of 'em," he says proudly.

"I bet you do."

"I give him a couple every time he comes in here. But . . . I guess he heard one too many. I don't think he has a very good sense of humor anyway," he says. "Most doctors don't."

"Or maybe he just wanted you to be straight with him," I say.

"Straight?"

"Straightforward," I say. "Just be your normal average guy and tell him what is bothering you, where it hurts."

"Ah," my father says. "As in, 'Doctor, doctor! I'm dying, please cure me.' Like that?"

"Like that," I say. "Sort of, but —"

"But we both know there is no cure for what I've got," he says, the smile diminishing, his body falling deeper into the bed, the old fragility returning. "Reminds me of the Great Plague of '33. No one knew what it was, or where it came from. One day everything seemed fine and the next — the

131

strongest man in Ashland: dead. Died while eating his breakfast. Rigor mortis set in so quick his body froze right there at the kitchen table, spoon lifted halfway to his mouth. After him, a dozen died in an hour. Somehow, I was immune. I watched my neighbors fall to the ground as though their bodies had become suddenly and irrevocably vacant, as if —"

"Dad," I say a couple of times, and when he finally stops I take his thin and brittle hand in my own. "No more stories, okay? No more stupid jokes."

"They're stupid?"

"I mean that in the nicest possible way."

"Thank you."

"Just for a little while," I say, "let's talk, okay? Man to man, father to son. No more stories."

"Stories? You think I tell stories? You wouldn't believe the stories my dad used to tell me. You think I tell *you* stories, when I was boy I heard *stories.* He'd wake me up in the middle of the night to tell me a story. It was awful."

"But even *that's* a story, Dad. I don't believe it for a minute."

"You're not necessarily supposed to *believe* it," he says wearily. "You're just supposed to believe in it. It's like — a metaphor."

"I forget," I say. "What's a metaphor?"

"Cows and sheep mostly," he says, wincing a bit as he says it.

"See?" I say. "Even when you're serious you can't keep from joking. It's frustrating, Dad. It keeps me at arm's length. It's like — you're scared of me or something."

"Scared of you?" he says, rolling his eyes. "I'm dying and I'm supposed to be scared of you?"

"Scared of getting close to me."

He takes this in, my old man, and looks away, into his past.

"It must have something to do with my father," he says. "My father was a drunk. I never told you that, did I? He was a terrible drunk, the worst kind. Sometimes he was too drunk to get it for himself. He had me get it for him for a while but then I stopped, refused. Finally, he taught his dog, Juniper, to go get it. Carried an empty bucket to the corner saloon and had him bring it back full of beer. Paid for it by sticking a dollar bill into the dog's collar. One day he didn't have any ones, all he had was a five, so he stuck that in his collar.

"The dog didn't come back. Drunk as he was, my father went down to the bar and found the dog sitting there on a stool, drinking a double martini.

"My dad was angry and hurt.

" 'You never did anything like this before,' my dad said to Juniper.

" 'I never had the money before,' Juniper said."

And he looks at me, unrepentant.

"You can't do it, can you?" I say, voice rising, teeth grinding.

"Sure I can," he says.

"Okay," I say. "Do it. Tell me something. Tell me about the place you come from."

"Ashland," he says, licking his lips.

"Ashland. What was it like?"

"Small," he says, mind drifting. "So small."

"How small?"

"It was so small," says he, "that when you plugged in an electric razor, the street light dimmed."

"Not a good start," I say.

"People were so cheap there," he says, "they ate beans to save on bubble bath."

"I love you, Dad," I say, getting closer to him. "We deserve better than this. But you're making this too hard. Help me, here. What were you like as a boy?"

"I was a fat boy," he says. "Nobody would ever play with me. I was so fat I could only play seek. That's how fat I was," he says, "so fat I had to make two trips just to leave the house," not smiling now because he's not trying to be funny, he is just being him, something he can't not be. Beneath one facade there's another facade and then another, and beneath that the aching dark place, his life, something that neither of us understands. All I can say is, "One more chance. I'll give you one more chance and then I'm leaving, I'm going, and I don't know if I'm coming back. I'm not going to be your straight man anymore."

And so he says to me, my father, the very father who is dying here in front of me, though today he looks good for someone in his condition, he says, "You're not yourself today son," in his best Groucho, winking just in case — and this is a long shot — I take him seriously, "and it's a great improvement."

But I do take him seriously; this is the problem. I stand to go but as I stand he grabs me by the wrist and holds me with a power I didn't think he had any longer. I look at him.

"I know when I'm going to die," he says, looking deep into my eyes. "I've seen it. I know when and how it's going to happen and it's not today, so don't worry."

He is completely serious, and I believe him. I actually believe him. He knows. I have a thousand thoughts in my head but can speak none of them. Our eyes are locked and I'm filled with a wonder. He knows.

"How do you — why —"

"I've always known," he says, softly, "always had this power, this vision. I've had it since I was a boy. When I was a boy I had a series of dreams. They woke me up screaming. My father came to me on the first night and asked me what was wrong and I told him. I told him I'd dreamed my aunt Stacy had died. He assured me that Aunt Stacy was fine and I went back to bed.

"But the next day she died.

"A week or so later the same thing happened. Another dream, I woke up screaming. He came to my room and asked me what had happened. I told him I dreamed Gramps had died. Again he told me — though with perhaps a bit of trepidation in his voice — that Gramps was fine, and so I went back to sleep.

"The next day, of course, Gramps died.

"For a few weeks I didn't have another dream. Then I did, I had another, and Father came and asked me what I had dreamed and I told him: I dreamed that my father had died. He of course assured me that he was fine and to think no more of it, but I could tell it rattled him, and I heard him pacing the floor all night, and the next

136

day he was not himself, always looking this way and that as if something was going to fall on his head, and he went into town early and was gone for a long time. When he came back he looked terrible, as if he had been waiting for the ax to fall all day.

" 'Good God,' he said to my mother when he saw her. 'I've had the worst day of my entire life!'

" 'You think *you've* had a bad day,' she says. 'The milkman dropped dead on the porch this morning!' "

I slam the door behind me when I leave, hoping he has a heart attack, dies quickly, so we can get this whole thing over with. I've already started grieving, after all.

"Hey!" I hear him call to me through the door. "Where's your sense of humor? And if not your sense of humor, your pity? Come back!" he calls to me. "Give me a break, son, please! I'm dying in here!"

The Day I Was Born

The day I was born Edward Bloom was listening to a football game on a transistor radio he had tucked into his shirt pocket. He was also mowing the lawn and smoking a cigarette. It had been a wet summer and the grass was high, but today the sun beat down on my father and my father's yard with an intensity recalling an earlier time when the sun was hotter, the way everything in the world used to be hotter or bigger or better or simpler than things were right about now. The tops of his shoulders were as red as an apple, but he didn't notice because he was listening to the biggest football game of the year, the one that pitted his school team, Auburn, against their nemesis, Alabama, a game that Alabama invariably won.

He thought of my mother, briefly, who was inside the house, looking at the electric bill. The house was as cold as an icebox, but still she was sweating.

She was sitting at the kitchen table looking at the electric bill when she felt me urging her along, dropping into position.

Soon, she thought, taking a breath in

quickly, but she didn't get up, or even stop looking at the bill. She just thought that one word. *Soon.*

Outside, as he mowed the lawn, it wasn't looking good for Auburn. Never did. It was the same every time: you went into the game believing that this was going to be the year they did it, this was going to be it, finally, and it never was.

It was almost halftime, and Auburn was already down ten.

On the day I was born, my father finished the front and then started the backyard with a renewed sense of optimism. In the second half Auburn came out charging and scored a touchdown on their first possession. Now down only three, anything was possible.

Alabama scored just as quickly, and then, off a fumble, they scored a field goal.

My mother placed the electric bill flat on the table, and pressed it with her hands as though trying to get out the wrinkles. She didn't know that all my father's hard work and perseverance would, in a matter of only a few days, pay off handsomely, and that she would never have to worry about an electric bill again. For now the world, the entire planetary solar system, seemed to orbit around the center that was this bill for $42.27. But she had to have the house cool. She was carrying around all this weight. Naturally she was a slim woman but she was as big as a house now with me inside her. And she liked it cool.

She heard my father in the backyard, mowing. Her eyes widened: I was coming. *Now.* I was coming now.

Auburn was making a comeback.

Time passed. She calmly gathered her hospital things. Auburn had the ball with but a few seconds remaining. Time for a field goal.

On the day I was born, my father stopped mowing the lawn and listened to the announcer's voice on the radio. He stood like a statue in his backyard, half of which had been mown, half to go. He knew they were going to lose.

On the day I was born, the world became a small and joyous place.

My mother screamed, my father screamed.

On the day I was born, they won.

How He Saw Me

I was unimpressive at first — small and pink, helpless, with no real skills to speak of. I couldn't even roll over. When my father was a boy, a child, a baby — he had brought more into the world with him than I did. Times were different then, and more was asked of everybody, even the babies. Even the babies had to pull their weight.

But as a baby I didn't know those hard times. Born in a real hospital, with the best medical care and all kinds of drugs for my mother, I just didn't know what birth was like in the old days. Though this didn't change anything: Edward loved me. He did. He'd always wanted a boy and here I was. He'd expected more, of course, from my arrival. A muted brilliance, a glow, maybe even a halo of some kind. That mystical feeling of completion. But none of that came. I was just a baby, like any other — except, of course, that I belonged to him, and that made me special. I cried a lot and slept a lot and that was about it; my repertoire was very limited, though there were those moments of peaceful clarity and joy when I stared up at my father from his lap, my eyes beaming, as though he were a god — which, in a way, he was. Or godlike anyway, having created this life, having planted the magic seed. At those times he could see how smart I was, how bright, he could visualize my potential in the world. So much was possible.

But then I would start to cry again, or my diaper would need changing, and he would have to hand me over to my mother who fixed all that and fed me, while Edward watched helplessly from his chair, suddenly tired, excruciatingly tired of the noise, the sleepless nights, the smell. Tired of his tired wife. So he missed the old life sometimes, the freedom, the time to think things through — but did that make him different from any other man? It was different with women, they were made to raise a family, they had the attention span for it. Men had to go out of the house and work, that's the way it had always been, from the time of the hunter-gatherers it was so and still was today. Men were torn in this way; they had to be two people, one at home and another away, while a mother had to be but one.

In those first weeks he took his job as father quite seriously. Everyone noticed: Edward had changed. He was more thoughtful, deeper, philosophical. While my mother took care of the day-to-day things, he brought vision to the task. He made a list of the virtues he possessed and wanted to pass on to me:

> perseverance
> ambition
> personality
> optimism
> strength
> intelligence
> imagination

Wrote it on the back of a paper bag. Virtues he'd had to discover himself, he'd be able to share with me, free of charge. Suddenly he saw what a great chance this was, how my empty-handed arrival was actually a blessing. Looking into my eyes he saw a great emptiness, a desire to be filled. And this would be his job, as father: filling me up.

Which he did on weekends. He wasn't there very often during the week, because he was on the road, selling, following money — working. Teaching by example. Were there jobs out there where a man could make a good living without traveling, without getting off his duff and moving, sleeping in hotels, and eating on the run out of to-go containers? Possibly. But they didn't suit him. The very idea of coming home at the same time every single day made him just a little nauseated. Regardless of how much he loved his wife, his son, he could only stand so much love. Being alone was lonely, but there was an even greater loneliness sometimes when he was surrounded by a lot of other people who were constantly making demands of him. He needed a break.

Coming home he felt like a stranger. Everything had changed. His wife had rearranged the living room, bought a new dress, made new friends, read strange books, which she brazenly placed on her bedside table. And I grew so quickly. His wife couldn't see it as clearly, but he could. Coming back he saw this incredible growth, and seeing it realized how much smaller this made him, relatively speaking. So in a way it was true: as I grew, he shrank. And by this logic one day I would become a giant, and Edward would become nothing, invisible in the world.

Before that could happen, though, before he disappeared, he was a father, and he did the things a father was supposed to do. He played some catch, he bought the bike. He packed lunch for the picnics to the mountain overlooking the town, the great city of endless promise, from which he could see the spot where he first did this, and then that, and over there where he made his first deal, and there where he kissed that pretty woman, and all the triumph and glory of his short life. This is what he saw when he went there, not the buildings or the skyline, not the tree groves or the hospital where they were building the new wing. No: it was his story, the story of his adult life spread out before him like a landscape, and he would take me there and hold me up so I could see and he would say, "Someday son, this will all be yours."

How He Saved My Life

Edward Bloom saved my life twice that I know of.

The first time I was five years old, and I was playing in the ditch behind our house. My father always told me, "Stay out of the ditch, William." He told me this again and again, as if he knew something might happen, that he might be forced to save my life one day. To me it wasn't a ditch, but some ancient half-dried riverbed, filled with prehistoric stones made flat and smooth by the water flowing over them through time. The only water there now was a constant, though almost negligible stream, not strong enough to carry a twig.

This is where I played, after I slid down the red clay embankment, sometimes merely minutes after my father might have told me, "Stay out of the ditch, William." The vision I had of myself, alone between the cool red walls, was powerful enough to override the command. In my secret place I would squat, turning over stone after stone, pocketing the best, the white ones, and the shiny black ones with the white spots. I was so transfixed there

146

that day that I failed to see the rushing wall of water coming for me, as if on a mission to sweep me up and take me away with it. I didn't see it and I didn't hear it. I was squatting with my back to it, looking at the stones. And had it not been for my father, who somehow knew what was happening before it happened, I would have gone away with it, too. But he was there, and he lifted me by my shirt tail up and out of the ditch, and onto the bank, where the two of us watched a river flow where no river had flowed before, its foamy crest spilling onto our very toes. Finally, he looked at me.

"I told you to stay out of the ditch," he said.

"What ditch?" I said.

The second time my father saved my life we had just moved to a new house on Mayfair Drive. The previous owner had left a swing set behind, and as the movers lugged in our old couches and dining-room table, I set my sights on seeing just how high that baby would go. I pumped with all I had, shaking the swing with the pulse of my power. Unfortunately, the previous owner hadn't left the swing behind; they had merely yet to take it. They had released the legs of the frame from the cement that anchored them to the ground, and so as I swung higher and higher I was actually taking the weight of the set itself with me, until, at the top of my highest arc, the set plunged forward, sending me out of the swing and on an unlikely trajectory toward a white picket fence, on which I would assuredly have been impaled. Suddenly I felt my father near me; it was as though he were flying, too, and that we were both falling together. His arms embraced me like a cloak, and I came to rest on the ground beside him. He had plucked me from Heaven and set me down safely on Earth.

His Immortality

My father gave me early indications that he would live forever.

One day he fell off the roof. The yardman had been cleaning the leaves from the gutter and, having gone home without quite finishing, had left the ladder leaning against the house. My father came home from the office, saw the ladder, and climbed it. He wanted to see what the view was from up there. He was, he said, curious to know whether or not he could see his tall office building from the top of our own house.

I was nine years old by then and I knew danger. I told him not to do it. I said it was dangerous. He stared at me for a long moment, and he winked, the wink meaning any goddamn thing I wanted it to mean.

Then he climbed the ladder. It was probably the first ladder he had climbed in ten years, but I can only suppose about that. Maybe he climbed ladders all the time. I wouldn't know.

After climbing the ladder he stood over by the chimney, turning in circles and staring south, north, east, and west for some sign of his building. He was handsome up there, dressed in his dark suit and shiny black shoes. He seemed finally to have found the place where he might be most advantageously displayed: at the top of a house two stories high. He walked — *strolled* — back and forth on the roof above me, a hand above his eyes like a ship's captain looking for land. But he could not see it. His office building remained invisible in the distance.

Then, suddenly, he fell, and I, I watched him fall. I watched my father falling off the roof of his own house. It happened so quickly I don't know whether he tripped or slipped or what — he may have jumped for all I know — but he fell two stories into a large bed of shrubbery. Until the last second I kept expecting him to grow wings, and when he didn't, when no wings came, I knew the fall had killed him. I was so sure he was dead I didn't even rush to his side to see what could be done to save him, to revive him, possibly.

I walked, slowly, to the body. He was completely still, not breathing. On his face was that expression of beatific slumber that one associates with release from this world. A pleasant expression. I stared at it, memorized it — my father, my father's face in death — when all of a sudden his face moved, he winked at me, laughed, and said, "Had you going there, didn't I?"

His Greatest Power

When Edward Bloom left Ashland he made a promise to himself that he would see the world, and thus it was that he seemed forever moving, and never in one place for too long. There was not a continent that his foot didn't touch, not a country that he didn't visit, not one great city in which he could not find a friend. He was a true man of the world. He made cameo and yet heroic appearances in my own life, saving my life when he could, urging me toward my own manhood. And yet he was called away by forces greater even than himself; he was, as he said, riding the tiger.

But he liked to leave me laughing. This is how he wanted to remember me, and how he wanted to be remembered. Of all his great powers, this was perhaps his most extraordinary: at any time, at the drop of a hat, he could really break me up.

There was this man — we'll call him Roger — who had to go out of town on business, and so left his cat in the care of a neighbor. Now, the man loved his cat, loved his cat beyond all things, so much so that the very night of the day he left he called his neighbor to inquire into the general health and emotional well-being of this dear feline. And so he asked his neighbor, "How is my sweet little darling precious cat? Tell me, neighbor, please."

And the neighbor said, "I'm sorry to have to tell you this, Roger. But your cat is dead. It was run over by a car. Killed instantly. Sorry."

Roger was shocked! And not merely at the news of his cat's demise — as if that weren't enough! — but also at the way in which he was told about it.

So he said, he said, "That's not the way you tell somebody about something as horrible as this! When something like this happens you tell the person slowly, you ease them into it. You prepare them! For instance. When I called this evening you should have said, Your cat's on the roof. Then the next time I call you would say, The cat's still on the roof, he won't come down and he's looking pretty sick. Then the next time I call you might tell me the cat fell off the roof and that he's now at the vet in intensive care. Then, then the next time I call you tell me — your voice sort of quivery and shaky — that he died. Got it?"

"Got it," said the neighbor. "Sorry."

So three days later Roger called the neighbor again, because his neighbor was still watching the house and checking his mail, et cetera, and Roger wanted to know if anything important had happened. And the neighbor said, "Yes. As a matter of fact, yes. Something important has happened."

"Well?" asked Roger.

"Well," the neighbor said. "It's about your father."

"My father!" exclaimed Roger. "My father! What about my father?"

"Your father," said the neighbor, "is on the roof . . ."

My father is on the roof. This is how I like to remember him sometimes. Well-dressed in a dark suit and shiny, slippery shoes, he is looking left, looking right, looking as far as his eyes will travel. Then, looking down, he sees me, and just as he begins his fall he smiles, and winks. All the way down he's looking at me — smiling, mysterious, mythic, an unknown quantity: my dad.

In Which He Has a Dream

My dying father has a dream that he is dying. At the same time, it is a dream about me.

It goes like this: as news of my father's illness spread, mourners began to gather in the yard, first just a few, but soon there were many, a dozen, then two, then half-a-hundred people, all standing around in the yard, ruining the shrubbery, crushing the monkey grass, huddling beneath the carport when it rained. Shoulder to shoulder in my father's dream they swayed and moaned, waiting for word of recovery. Barring that, a glimpse of my father at the bathroom window as he passed before it sent up a wild and glorious cheer. My mother and I watched from the living-room window, unsure of what to do. Some of the mourners looked poor. They wore old, ragged clothes and their faces were dark with hair. They made my mother feel uneasy; she fingered the buttons on her blouse as she watched them stare sadly at the second-floor windows. But there were others who looked as if they had left some very important job to come to my father's house and mourn. They had removed their ties and stuffed them in their pockets, the sides of their fine black shoes were rimmed with mud, and some of them had portable phones, which they used to communicate the proceedings to those who couldn't be here. Men and women, young and old alike all looked upward toward the light of my father's window, waiting. Nothing really happened for a long time. I mean, it was just our life, with the people outside in the yard. But the fact of it became too much, and after a few weeks of it my mother asked me to ask them to go.

And so I did. By this time, though, they were entrenched. A rudimentary buffet had been established beneath the magnolia, where they served bread and chili and steamed broccoli. They kept bothering my mother for forks and spoons, which were returned with the chili still on them, cold and hard to remove. A small tent city had appeared on the patch of open grass where I used to play touch football with some of the neighborhood kids, and word had it that a baby had been born there. One of the businessmen with the portable phones had set up a small information center on a tree stump, and people came to him if they wanted to get messages out to loved ones far away, or to find out if there had been any news of my father.

But in the middle of it all sat an older man in a lawn chair, overseeing everything. I'd never seen him before to my knowledge (or so went my father's dream) but he looked somehow familiar — a stranger, and yet no foreigner to me. Occasionally someone came to him and said something close to his ear. He would listen thoughtfully, consider for a moment what the man had said, and then either nod or shake his head. He had a thick white beard and glasses, and he wore a fishing cap, in which several handmade lures were pinned. And so as he seemed to be some kind of leader, I went to see him first.

There was someone whispering to him as I approached, and as I opened my mouth to speak he raised a hand to quiet me. After the man had finished speaking the old man shook his head, and the messenger hurried off. Then the old man lowered his hand and looked at me.

"Hello," I said. "I'm —"

"I know who you are," he said. His voice was soft and deep, warm and distant at the same time. "You are his son."

"That's right," I said.

We looked at each other, and as we did I tried to recall a name, for surely we had met somewhere before. But nothing came.

"You have some word for us?"

He watched me with rapt attention, almost seizing me with his stare. He was a most imposing man, my father told me.

"None," I said. "I mean, he's about the same, I guess."

"The same," the man said, weighing the words carefully as if to derive some special meaning. "He's still swimming, then?"

"Yes," I said. "Every day. He really loves it."

"This is good," he said. And suddenly he raised his voice and shouted, "He is still swimming!" And a great cry of rejoicing arose from the crowd. The man's face was radiant. For a few moments he breathed deeply through his nose, and seemed to think things over. Then he looked at me again.

"But there's something else you came to tell us, isn't there?"

"There is," I said. "It's just that, I know you mean well, and you all seem very nice. But I'm afraid that —"

"We must go," the man said calmly. "You want us to leave."

"Yes," I said. "I'm afraid so."

The old man took this in. His head seemed to nod briefly, as if it were moved by the news. This is the scene my father watched in his dream, as if, he said, from a distance, as though he were already dead.

"It will be hard," the old man said, "to go. These people — they really care. They'll be lost without this place. Not for long, of course. Lives have a way of getting on with themselves. But in the short run it will be hard. Your mother —"

"It makes her nervous," I said. "All these people in the yard, day and night. You can understand that."

"Of course," he said. "And there's the mess, too. We've almost completely destroyed the front yard."

"There is that."

"Not to worry," he said, in a way that made me believe him. "We shall leave it as we found it."

"She'll be pleased."

A woman ran up to me then and grabbed my shirt in her hands and rubbed her sobbing face against it, as if to determine my corporeality.

"William Bloom?" she said, and looked at me imploringly. She was a small woman, with thin wrists. "You *are* William Bloom, aren't you?"

"Yes," I said, moving back a step or two, but she still clung to me. "I am."

"Give this to your father," she said, and thrust into my hand a miniature silk pillow.

"Healing herbs in a little pillow," she said. "I made it myself. They might help."

"Thank you," I said. "I'll see to it he gets them."

"He saved my life, you know," she said. "There was a great fire. He risked his own life to save mine. And here — here I am today."

"Not for long," the old man said. "He's asked us to leave."

"Edward?" she said. "Edward Bloom has asked us to leave?"

"No," he said. "His wife and son."

She nodded.

"As you said it would be," she said. "The son would come to us and ask us to leave. It is just as you said."

"My mother asked me to," I said, becoming frustrated with the mysterious talk and sly innuendo. "This is not something I enjoy."

And suddenly there was a great collective gasp. Everyone was looking toward the windows on the second floor, where my father stood waving at the people in his dream. He was in his yellow bathrobe, smiling at them, occasionally picking someone out in the crowd he recognized and pointing, raising his eyebrows, and mouthing a word or two — *Are you okay? Good to see you!* — before moving on to someone else. Everyone waved, shouted, cheered, and then, after what seemed a visit of immensely brief proportions, he waved once again, and turned, and disappeared into the semidarkness of his room.

"Well," the old man said, beaming, "that was something, wasn't it? He looked good. He looked very good."

"You're taking good care of him," a woman said.

"Keep up the good work!"

"I owe everything to your father!" someone called to me from beneath the magnolia, and what followed was a cacophony of voices, pure babble, telling some story or other about Edward Bloom and his good deeds. I felt surrounded by all the words. Then I felt surrounded: a converging line had formed around me, people talking all at once, until the old man raised his hand and shushed them, and they backed away.

"See," the old man said. "We all have stories, just as you do. Ways in which he touched us, helped us, gave us jobs, lent us money, sold it to us wholesale. Lots of stories, big and small. They all add up. Over a lifetime it all adds up. That's why we're here,

William. We're a part of him, of who he is, just as he is a part of us. You still don't understand, do you?"

I didn't. But as I stared at the man and he stared back at me, in my father's dream I remembered where we'd met before.

"And what did my father do for you?" I asked him, and the old man smiled.

"He made me laugh," he said.

And I knew. In the dream, my father told me, I knew. And with that I walked through the yard and down the walk and back into the warmth of my glowing home. "Why does an elephant have a trunk?" I heard the old man bellow in his strong, deep voice, just as I closed the door. "Because he doesn't have a glove compartment," I mouthed along with him.

Followed by a great burst of laughter.

Thus ends my dying father's dream about his death.

III

In Which He Buys a Town, and More

This next story rises from the mist of the past like a shadow.

Hard work, good luck, and a number of canny investments make my father a wealthy man. We move to a bigger house, a nicer street, and my mother stays at home and raises me, and as I grow my father continues to work hard as ever. He is gone weeks at a time, and comes home tired and sad, with little to say other than he missed us.

Thus, despite his great success no one seems happy. Not my mother, not me, and certainly not my father. There is even talk of disbanding the family altogether, it looks and acts so unlike one. But this doesn't happen. Opportunities come in disguise sometimes. My parents decide to see the hard times through.

It is during these times, the mid-seventies, when my father begins to spend his money in unpredictable ways. One day he realizes that there is something missing in his life. Or rather it's a feeling that comes over him slowly as he ages — he'd just turned forty —

until one day he finds himself, quite by accident, stuck. In a little town called Specter. Specter, a town somewhere in Alabama or Mississippi or Georgia. Stuck there because his car has broken down. He has his car towed to a mechanic, and while he waits for it to be fixed, he decides to take a walk around.

Specter, not surprisingly, turns out to be a beautiful little town full of small white houses, porches and swings, beneath trees as big as all time to give them shade. And here and there are flower boxes and flower gardens, and in addition to a fine-looking Main Street there's a nice mix of dirt, gravel, and asphalt roads, all of them nicely drivable. My father takes special note of these roads as he walks because, more than anything else, this is what my father loves to do. Drive. Past things. To get in cars and drive down roads all over the country, all over the world, to drive just as slowly as the law will allow — although the law, especially as it pertains to speed limits, is not something Edward Bloom respects: twenty in town is too fast for him; the highways are madness. How can the world be seen at such speeds? Where do people need to go so badly they can't realize what is already here, outside the car window? My father remembers when there were no cars at all. He remembers when people used to walk. And he does, too — walk, that is — but he still loves the feeling of an engine rumbling, wheels rolling, the display of life framed in the windows in front and back and on all sides. The car is my father's magic carpet.

Not only does it get him places, but it shows him places. A car . . . he drives, is driven, so slowly, and takes so long to get from here to there that some of his important business deals are done in cars. Those who have appointments with him follow this procedure: they find out where he is on this or that day, and figure that, being such a slow driver, he will remain in the general vicinity for most of the rest of the week, then they fly to the closest airport and rent a car. From there they hit the road and drive until they catch up with him. They will drive up beside his car and honk and wave, and my father will slowly turn — the way Abraham Lincoln would have slowly turned if Lincoln had ever driven a car, because in my mind — in the memory that has lodged itself imperturbably in my mind, my father resembles Abraham Lincoln, a man with long arms and deep pockets and dark eyes — and he waves back, and pulls over, and whoever needs to speak to him gets in on the passenger side, and this person's deputies or lawyers will get in the back, and as they continue to drive along these beautiful wandering roads their business is done. And who knows? Maybe he even has affairs in these cars, romances with beautiful women, famous actresses. At night a small table is set between them, covered in a white tablecloth, and, by candle light, they eat and drink, and make frivolous toasts to the future . . .

In Specter my father walks. It happens to be a nice fall day. He smiles at everything and everyone gently, and everything and everyone smiles gently back. He walks with his hands clasped behind him, peering with a friendly gaze into storefronts and alleyways, and already by this time somewhat sensitive to the sun's light, squinting therefore, which only makes him seem friendlier, and more delicate, which he is: he is friendlier and certainly more delicate than he seems, ever, to anyone. And he falls in love with this town, with its marvelous simplicity, its unadorned charm, the people who greet him, who sell him a Coke, who wave to him and smile at him from their cool porches as he passes.

My father decides to buy this town. Specter has that special somber quality, he says to himself, a quality not unlike living under water, that he can appreciate. It is a sad place, actually, and has been for years, since the railroad was shut down. Or the coal mines dried up. Or the way it seems that Specter has just been forgotten, that the world has passed it by. And though Specter did not have much use for the world anymore, it would have been nice to be part of it, to have been invited.

This is the quality my father falls in love with, and this is the reason he makes the town his own.

The first thing he does is to purchase all the land surrounding Specter, as a kind of buffer, in case some other rich, suddenly lonely man stumbles upon the town and wants to build a highway through it. He doesn't even look at the land; he only knows that it's green with pine and that he wants to keep it that way, wants what is, in effect, a self-enclosed ecosystem. And he gets it. No one knows one man is buying the hundreds of tiny parcels that are up for sale, just as no one knows it when every house and store in town is bought, one by one, over a period of about five or six years, by someone other than anybody somebody else knows. Not for a while anyway. There are people who are moving, and there are businesses that are closing, and these are not difficult to purchase at all, but to those who like things fine just as they are and who want to stay in one place, a letter is sent. The letter offers to buy their property and everything on it for a handsome price. They are not asked to leave, to pay rent, or to change anything but the name in which the house — every house — and store — every store — is owned.

And in just this way, slowly but quite surely, my father buys Specter. Every square inch of it.

I imagine him quite pleased with the transaction.

For, true to his word, nothing changes, nothing but the sudden and suddenly routine appearance in town of my father, Edward Bloom. He does not call in advance, for I don't believe even he knows when he's going to make it back, but one day he will be seen by somebody. He is the lone figure standing out in the fields, or the one walking down Ninth Street with his hands deep in his pockets. He walks through the stores he now owns and breaks a dollar or two, but he leaves the management of these stores to the men and women of Specter, of whom he will ask, in his soft, grandfatherly voice, *Well, now, how are things? And how is your wife, the kids?*

He clearly loves the town so much, and all of the people in it, and they love him back, because it is impossible not to love my father.

Impossible. This, anyway, is what I imagine: it is impossible not to love my father.

Fine, Mr. Bloom. Everything's just fine. We had a good month last month. Would you like to see the books? But he shakes his head, no. *I'm sure you have everything well under control here. Just stopped in to say hello. Well, I've got to go now. Good-bye. Say hello to your wife for me, would you?*

And when the high school boys of Specter play baseball against other teams from other schools, he might be seen — his tall dark gauntness — alone in the stands in his three-piece suit, watching the proceedings with the proud, detached quality with which he watched me grow.

Each time he comes to Specter he stays with a different family. No one knows who it will be, or when, but there is always a room ready for him when he asks, and he always asks, as though it will be as a favor to a stranger. *Please, if it wouldn't be too much trouble.* And he will eat with the family and sleep in the room and in the morning be on his way. And he always makes his bed.

"I reckon Mr. Bloom will have himself a soda on a day as hot as this one," Al says to him one day. "Let me get one for you, Mr. Bloom."

"Thank you, Al," my father says. "That will be fine, actually. A soda will be fine."

He sits on a bench in front of Al's Country Store, doing nothing. Al's Country Store — he smiles at the name, and tries to cool down in the shade beneath the overhang. Just the tips of his black shoes jut out into the bright sunlight of this summer's day. Al brings him the soda. Another man named Wiley is there, and this old man chews on the end of a pencil, and stares at my father as he drinks. Wiley had been the sheriff in Specter for a while, then the pastor. After being the pastor he became the grocer, but by this time, talking to my father in front of Al's Country Store, he does nothing at all. He is retired from everything but talking.

Wiley says, "Mr. Bloom, I know I've said it before. I know I have. But I will say it again. It is great what you've done with this town."

My father smiles.

"I haven't done anything with this town, Wiley."

"That's just it!" Wiley says, and laughs, and Al laughs, and my father laughs, too. "We think that's great."

"How is that soda, Mr. Bloom?"

"Refreshing," my father says. "It's quite refreshing, Al. Thank you."

Wiley has a farm a mile out of town. It is one of the first worthless things my father ever bought.

"I have to say what Wiley says," Al says. "Not every man could come and buy a whole town for the love of it."

My father's eyes are almost closed; it won't be long now before he can't go outside without powerful sunglasses on, his eyes become so sensitive to the light. But he can accept these good words with grace.

"Thank you, Al," he says. "When I saw Specter, I knew I had to have it. I don't know why except to say it's so. I had to have it all. I suppose in part it has to do with circles, with entireties. It is very difficult for a man such as myself to settle for a piece of something. If part of something is good, the whole of it can only be better. And as far as Specter is concerned, this is certainly the case. To have it all —"

"But you don't," Wiley says, still chewing on his pencil. His eyes move from Al to my father.

"Wiley," Al says.

"Well, it's the truth!" he says. "Can't be wrong to say it if it's so."

My father turns to Wiley slowly, because my father has this special talent: just by looking at a man he can tell what the man's motivation is in saying a thing, whether or not he is honest or true or trying for more than is right. It's a kind of power, and it's one of the reasons he became so rich.

And he can tell that Wiley thinks he is telling the truth.

"Well, that can't be, Wiley," he says. "That is, not as far as I know. I've been over every inch of this town either on foot or in my car, or seen it from the air, and I feel sure I've purchased it all. In its entirety. The whole kit and caboodle. It's a perfect circle."

"Fine then," Wiley says. "I won't bring up that patch of ground with the shack on it between where the road stops and the lake starts that just might be hard to find by foot or car or to see from the air, and just might not be on any map, or how whoever owns it has a piece of paper you've never seen to sign, Mr. Bloom. Because you and Al have all the truth with you over there. Don't know what I'm talking about, I guess. My apologies to you who knows better."

Wiley is kind enough to tell my father how to get there, how the road seems to end where it doesn't, and how the lake seems to be where it isn't, and how hard it would be for anybody to think to find this strange place: a swamp. A shack in a swamp. And so my father drives until the road seems to end, but when he gets out of his car it's clear that beyond the trees and vines and dirt and grass, the road is there, the road goes on. It has been reclaimed by nature, by the lake now too high for its own banks. In three inches of swamp water is more stagnant life than an ocean could hold; at its edge, where the muck hardens and warms, life itself begins. He walks into it. The swamp swallows up my father's shoes. He keeps walking. The water rises, the ooze clings to his trousers as he sinks. It feels good.

He keeps walking, no trouble seeing in the dim light. And all of a sudden there is a house ahead — a house. He can't believe that such a thing remains upright, that any weight will not be taken down in this soft earth, but there it is, not a shack at all but a real home, small but clearly well built, with four good sides and smoke coming out of a chimney. As he approaches the waters draw back, the ground hardens, a path is there for him to follow. And he thinks, smiling, how clever, and how lifelike: a path is provided at the very last moment, when one needs it least.

On one side of the house is a garden, and on the other there are wood piles as tall as he is himself. In a window box, a row of yellow flowers.

He makes his way to the door and knocks.

"Hello!" he calls out. "Is anybody home?"

"Sure," a young woman's voice calls back.

"May I come in?"

There's a pause, and then, "Wipe your feet on the mat."

My father does just that. He pushes the door gently open and stands there, looking around at what is an impossible cleanliness and order: in the middle of the blackest backwater he has ever seen, he is staring at a warm, clean, comfortable room. He sees the fire first, but quickly looks away. From there he glances at the mantle, on which there are a number of blue glass jars arranged in pairs, and from there he looks to the walls, which are nearly bare.

There is a small couch, two chairs, and a brown hearth rug.

In the doorway leading to another room stands the girl. She has long black hair braided in the back, and still blue eyes. She can't be more than twenty. Living in this swamp he would have expected her to be as covered in grime as he is now, but other than a streak of black ash across one side of her neck, her white skin and her cotton calico dress could scarcely be cleaner.

"Edward Bloom," she says. "You are Ed Bloom, aren't you?"

"Yes," he says. "How did you know?"

"Figured," she says. "I mean, who else?"

He nods and says that he is sorry to bother her and her family, but that he has come on business. He tells her he would like to speak to the owner of the house here — her father, mother? — and of the land the house is on.

She tells him he is doing just that.

"I'm sorry?"

"This is mine," she says.

"You?" he says. "But you're just a —"

"Woman," she says. "Near about."

"I'm sorry," my father says. "I don't mean —"

"Business, Mr. Bloom," she says, faintly smiling. "You said something about some business."

"Oh, yes," he says.

And he tells her everything he knows, how he came to Specter, how he fell in love with it, and how he merely wants to have it all. Call it a flaw in his nature if you will but he wants it, all of it, and this apparently is a piece of land he had overlooked, that he would like to buy it from her if she wouldn't mind, that nothing will change, she can stay here forever if she likes, he only wishes to call this town his own.

And she says, "Now let me get this straight. You'll buy this swamp from me, but

I'll stay in it. You'll own the house, but it'll still be mine. I'll be here, and you'll come and go as you please to one place or another because there's a flaw in your nature. Do I have that right?" And when he tells her that she does, that in so many words she has it right, she says, "Then I don't think so, Mr. Bloom. If nothing is going to change, I'd just as soon they not change the way things haven't been changing all this time."

"But you don't understand," he says. "In essence you will lose nothing. Everybody actually gains by this. Don't you see? You can ask anybody in Specter. I have been nothing if not beneficent. In every way, the people of Specter have profited by my presence here."

"Let them profit," she says.

"It's a small thing, really. I wish you'd reconsider." He's about to lose his temper, or break down in sadness. "I only want the best for everybody."

"Especially you," she says.

"For everybody," he says. "Including me."

She stares at my father for a long time, and shakes her head, her blue eyes still and steady.

"I don't have any folks, Mr. Bloom," she says. "They've been gone a long time." She gives him a cold, mean stare. "I've been fine here. I know things — well, you might be surprised at all I know. It's not like some big check is going to change anything for me. Money — I just don't need it. I don't need anything, Mr. Bloom. I'm happy the way things are."

"Young woman," my father asks, incredulous, "what is your name?"

"Jenny," she says, in a softer voice than the one she has been using till now. "My name is Jenny Hill."

The story goes like this: he falls in love with Specter first, then he falls in love with Jenny Hill.

Love is strange. What makes a woman like Jenny Hill suddenly decide my father is the man for her? What does he do to her? Is it that fabled charm? Or are Jenny Hill and Edward Bloom somehow made for each other? Did my father wait forty years and Jenny Hill twenty to finally find the loves of their lives?

I don't know.

On his shoulders he brings Jenny out of the swamp, and they drive to town together in his car. He drives so slowly at times that it is quite possible to walk beside his car at a good pace and talk to him, or, as it happens today, for all of Specter to line the sidewalks to see what he has with him now, to see the lovely Jenny Hill.

From the beginning of his stay in Specter, my father has maintained a small, white, black-shuttered home not far from the town park, on a street as pretty as spring, with a soft green lawn in front and a rose garden to one side, and an old barn converted to a garage on the other. There is a red wooden bird perched high on a white picket fence, whose wings whirl when the wind blows, and a straw mat on the front porch with the word *Home* woven into it.

And yet he has never stayed there. Not in the five years since he fell in love with Specter has he ever spent the night at the only house in town where no one else lives. Until he brings Jenny in from the swamp, he always stays with others. But now, with Jenny installed in the little white house with the soft green lawn not far from the park, he stays with her. He no longer surprises the people of Specter with his shy knock at dusk ("It's Mr. Bloom!" the kids scream, and jump all over him like a long lost uncle). He has a place of his own to stay now, and though at first some feelings are hurt, and the seemliness of the situation questioned by a few, pretty soon everybody sees the wisdom of living with the woman you love in the town you loved to live in. *Wise:* that's how they thought of my father from day one. He is wise and good and kind. If he does something that seems strange — such as going to a swamp to buy some land, and finding instead this woman — then that's because the rest of everybody just isn't as wise and kind and as good as he. And so pretty soon no one thinks twice about Jenny Hill, not in any small-minded way, that is, but rather merely to wonder how she holds up when Edward is gone, which, even the most forgiving of those in Specter will have to admit, is generally most of the time.

They wonder, *Isn't she lonely? What does she do with herself?* Things like that.

Jenny takes part in the life of the town, though. She helps organize events at school and is in charge of the cakewalk each fall at the local fair the town puts on. After so long in the swamp, keeping her lawn nice and green is no problem for her, and the garden just seems to thrive under her hand. But there are nights her neighbors hear her wail from a place deep inside herself, and, as if he can hear her, too, the next day or maybe the day after that he will be seen driving slowly through town, waving at everybody, and pulling up finally into the drive of the little house, where he will wave to the woman he loves, who might be standing on the porch, wiping her hands on her apron, a smile as big as the sun on her lovely face, her head just slightly shaking, and a soft *Hello*, almost as though he had never left at all.

Which, in fact, is how everybody comes to see him after a while. So many years have come and gone since he bought those first tracts of land on the outskirts of town, and so many more since he became a common presence, that people actually begin to take him for granted. His appearance in Specter is fantastic one day, quotidian the next. He owns every inch of land in town, and has been over every inch of it on his own as well. He has slept in every home and has visited every business; he remembers everybody's name, and everybody's dog's name, and how old the kids are, and when a big birthday is coming. It is the kids, of course, those who grow up seeing Edward around, who first accept him as they do any other natural phenomenon, as any other regular thing, and it carries over to the adults. A month will pass without him here, and then a day will come, bringing Edward with it. That old slow car of his — what a sight! *Hello, Edward! See you again soon. My best to Jenny. Come by the store.* And so many years began to pass in just this fashion, and his presence there becomes so ordinary and predictable that eventually it isn't as though he has never left, but as though he had never come in the first place. To everybody in that wonderful little town, from the youngest boy and girl to the oldest man, it is just like Edward Bloom has lived there all his life.

In Specter, history becomes what never happened. People mess things up, forget and remember all the wrong things. What's left is fiction. Though they never marry, Jenny becomes his young wife, Edward a kind of traveling salesman. People like to imagine how they must have met. The day he came through town so many years ago and saw her — where? — with her mother in the market? *Edward couldn't take his eyes off her. Followed her around all day.* Or is she rather the woman — the little girl? — who asked to wash his car for a nickel that day and who from that day on has set her sights on this man and told everybody who will listen, *He's mine. The day I turn twenty years old I'm going to make him marry me.* And sure enough, the day she turned twenty, she found Edward Bloom on the porch in front of the country store, rocking with Willard and Wiley and the rest, and though they had yet even to share a sentence together all she had to do was hold out her hand to be taken, and he took it, and they walked off together, and the next time anyone saw them they were man and wife, man and wife, and just about ready to move into that perfect little house near the park with the garden. Or maybe . . .

It doesn't matter; the story keeps changing. All of the stories do. Since none of them are true to begin with, the townspeople's memories take on a peculiar tint, their voices loud in the morning when, during the night, they might have remembered something else that never happened, a story good enough to share with the others, a new twist, a lie compounded daily. In the heat of a summer morning Willard might tell of the day — who could ever forget it? — when Edward was just a ten-year-old boy and the river (gone now, dried up, not there if you looked) rose so high that everyone feared that another drop from the black sky would wash away the town, another drop of rain falling into that mad river, and Specter would be no more. No one could forget how Edward started singing — he had that high, cool voice — and walking away, singing and walking away from town — and how the rain followed. How not another drop fell into the river, because the clouds followed him. He

184

charmed the falling water, and the sun came out, and Edward didn't come back until the rain was somewhere near Tennessee, and Specter was safe. Who could forget that?

Is any man ever kinder to animals than Edward Bloom? somebody might offer. *If there is one, show him to me; I'd like to see him. Because I remember when Edward was just a teenager and he was just so kind to the animals, all of them . . .*

Edward isn't in Specter all that often, of course; once a month for a couple of days at best. Although the truth is that their rich new landlord arrived there one afternoon with a broken down car, one afternoon after forty years of his life had already gone by, the townspeople do what they've always done — make things up — but now, instead of the simple fish stories that had satisfied them before, it is the history of the life Edward Bloom never lived in Specter that engages them, a life they wished they had, and the life, finally, he came to live in their minds: as Edward Bloom reinvented them, so they reinvented him.

And he seems to think this is a pretty good idea himself.

That is, he didn't seem to mind.

But that's another story. In this one,

things don't go so well with Jenny. It has to happen, doesn't it? A young woman just out of the swamp, and beautiful, as beautiful as anybody ever is, left all alone for so long. Oh the dark hours in which her youth is spent! She loves Edward Bloom — and who can blame her? No one doesn't love him. But he, Edward, he has the key to her heart, and he keeps it with him when he's gone.

There is something a little strange about Jenny, everybody begins to notice. The way she sits by the window now day and night staring out. People pass by and they wave but she can't see them. What she's looking at is far away. Her eyes glow. She doesn't blink. And this time Edward's gone for a long time, longer than before. Everybody misses him, of course, but Jenny especially. Jenny misses him the most, and this brings out the strange parts.

It's something somebody might have mentioned to Edward when he brought her in, the differentness about her. But no one there seemed to know Jenny Hill or her folks. Nobody. Yet how had she lived out in that swamp for twenty years without a soul knowing? Can this be?

No, it can't. But maybe nobody mentioned this to Edward because it didn't seem right. He was so happy. She seemed like a nice enough young woman at the time. And she was.

But no longer. No one can see Jenny Hill all cold and hard at the picture window staring out and think *nice*. They think, *There's a woman who's in no mood to be nice.* And her eyes glow. Really and truly. People go by the house at night and they swear they can see faint yellow lights at the window, two of them, her eyes, glowing in her head. And it's kind of scary.

Of course, the garden goes to hell in a hand basket. Weeds and vines overtake the rose bushes, finally strangling the life out of them. The grass in the yard grows, rises and falls from its own weight. A neighbor feels like helping her out with the yard, but when he goes over and knocks on her door, she doesn't answer.

Then what happens happens too quickly for anybody to act, mesmerized as they are by the despair emanating from the little white house. But in a matter of days the vines grow from one side of the house to the other, finally covering it over until it's hard to know there is a house there at all.

Then it rains. It rains for days and days. The lake rises, the dam almost bursts, and water begins to collect in the yard around Jenny's house. Small pools at first but the small pools meet, grow, and finally encircle her. The edge of the pool spills out into the street, and washes in close to the house next door. Water snakes find the big pool and thrive there, and trees whose roots can't cling to the shallow soil fall. Turtles rest on the trees, and moss grows thick on their trunks. Birds no one has seen before come and nest in the chimney of Jenny's house, and at night strange animal sounds can be heard coming from that deep dark place, sounds that keep most of the town shaking in their beds.

The swamp stops growing after a certain point, when the house is surrounded on all sides by yards of deep, dark, mossy water. And my father returns, finally, and sees what has happened, but by this time the swamp is too deep, the house too far away, and though he sees her glowing there he can't have her, and so he has to come back to us. The wandering hero returns, he always comes back to us. But when he leaves on business this is where he goes, this is still where he goes every time, and he calls to her but she won't speak. He can no longer have her, and that is why he is so sad and tired when he comes home, and why he has so little to say.

How It Ends

The ending is always a surprise. Even I was surprised by the ending.

I was in the kitchen making a peanut butter and jelly sandwich. My mother was cleaning the dust from the tops of the window frames, dust that you never see unless you step on a ladder and look, which is what she was doing, and I remember thinking what a sad and horrible life she must lead, to spend even a moment of it cleaning up these dusty distant frames, when my father came in. This was around four in the afternoon, which was strange because I couldn't remember the last time I'd even seen him when the sun was up, and looking at him in the full light I saw why: he didn't look so good. He looked terrible, in fact. He dropped something on the dining-room table and walked into the kitchen, his hard-soled shoes clicking against newly polished floor. My mother heard him, and as he stepped into the kitchen she stepped gingerly down, and dropped the cloth she was using on the counter beside the bread basket, and turned to look at him with what

I could only characterize as a look of desperation. She knew what he was about to tell her, tell us. She knew because he had been undergoing all these tests and biopsies, the nature of which they felt in their wisdom was best kept from me until they knew for certain, and they knew for sure today. That's why she had been dusting the tops of the windows, because today was the day they would know and she hadn't wanted to think about it, hadn't wanted to sit there thinking of nothing else but what she might learn today.

So she learned.

"It's everywhere," he said. That was it. *It's everywhere,* he said, and turned to leave, my mother following him quickly, leaving me to wonder what, besides God, was everywhere, and why it upset my parents so. But I didn't have to wonder long.

I figured it out before they even told me.

However, he did not die. Not yet. Instead of dying, he became a swimmer. We'd had a pool for years but he'd never really taken to it. Now that he was at home all the time and needing the exercise, he took to the pool as though he had been born in water, as though it were his natural element. And he was beautiful to watch. He cut through the water without seeming to displace it at all. His long pink body, covered in scars, lesions, bruises, and abrasions, shimmered in the reflecting blue. His arms swept in front of him with such sincerity, it was as if he were caressing the water instead of using it to move in. His legs moved with froglike precision behind him, and his head dipped below and broke the surface like a kiss. This went on for hours. Submerged for so long his skin soaked the water in and turned his wrinkles pure white; once I saw him peeling away this skin in chunky sheets, slowly, methodically, molting. Most of the rest of the day he slept. When he wasn't sleeping I sometimes caught him staring off, as if in communion with a secret. Watching him, he grew more foreign every day, and not just foreign to me, but a foreigner in this place and time. The way his eyes sank into his head, bereft of fire and passion. The way his body shrank and wilted. The way he seemed to be listening to a voice only he could hear.

I took some solace from the fact that all of this was happening for the good, that a happy ending would somehow occur, and that even this illness was a metaphor for something else: it meant that he was growing weary of the world. It had become so plain. No more giants, no all-seeing glass eyes, no more river-girls whose lives you could save, and who could come back later and save your own. He had become simply Edward Bloom: Man. I'd caught him at a bad time in his life. And this was no fault of his own. It was simply that the world no longer held the magic that allowed him to live grandly within it.

His illness was his ticket to a better place. I know this now.

Still, it was the best thing that could have happened to us, this final journey. Well, maybe not the *best* thing, but a good thing, all things considered. I saw him once every evening — more than I saw him when he was well. But he was the same old man, even then. Sense of humor: intact. I don't know why this seems important, but it does. I suppose in some cases it points to a certain resiliency, a strength of purpose, the spirit of an indomitable will.

A man was talking to a grasshopper. The man said, "You know, they have a drink named after you." And the grasshopper said, "You mean they have a drink named Howard?"

And this one. A man went into a restaurant and ordered a cup of coffee without cream. The waiter came back a few minutes later and told him he was sorry, they were all out of cream. Would he mind taking his coffee without milk?

But they were not even very funny anymore. We were simply waiting for the last day. We were telling the old, bad jokes, biding our time until the end came. He grew more and more weary. In the middle of a joke sometimes he'd forget what he was saying, or he'd give the wrong punch line — a great punch line, but a punch line that belonged to a different joke.

The pool itself began to deteriorate. No one took care of it after a while. We were too immobilized with the contemplation of the end of my father. Nobody cleaned it or added the special chemicals that kept the water blue, and algae began to grow on the walls, turning it a deep, thick green. But Dad kept swimming in it up until the end. Even when it began to look more like a pond than a pool, he kept swimming. One day when I went out to check on him, I could have sworn I saw a fish — a small-mouth bass, I thought — break the surface for a fly. I was sure of it.

"Dad?" I said. "Did you see that?"

He had paused midstroke and was floating on top of the water.

"Did you see that fish, Dad?"

But then I laughed because I looked at my father, teller of jokes, eternal comic, and saw that he looked *funny*. That's exactly what I thought, as I looked at him I thought, *He looks funny*. And sure enough, he hadn't paused mid-stroke at all. He had passed out, and his lungs had filled with water. I pulled him out of the pool and called for an ambulance. I pushed on his stomach and the water poured from his mouth as from a spigot. I waited for him to open an eye and wink, start laughing, turn this real-life event into something that it wasn't, into something truly awful and funny, something to look back on and laugh about. I held his hand and waited.

I waited a long time.

My Father's Death: *Take 4*

And so, finally, it happened like this.

Stop me if you've heard this one.

My father was dying. Sheltered inside an oxygen tent at Jefferson Memorial Hospital, his small, emaciated body seemed bleak and translucent, a kind of ghost already, even then. Mother waited with me, but would leave to talk to the doctors, or take walks because her back was hurting, and that would leave me alone with my father, and sometimes I'd take his hand, and wait.

The doctors, of which there were so many one referred to them as a "team," were all very grave, even hopeless. There was a Dr. Knowles, a Dr. Millhauser, a Dr. Vincetti. Each was a specialist famous in his field. Each kept an eye on that part of my father that was his specialty, and reported his findings to Dr. Bennett, our old family doctor, who, as captain of the team, was a generalist. He synthesized the details of their ongoing reports, filled in whatever blanks they may have left out, whereupon he would give us the Big Picture. He sometimes flattered us by using the words he had gone to school to learn: renal failure, for instance, and chronic hemolytic anemia. This last, this anemia, he described as being particularly debilitating, as the body retained excessive amounts of iron, creating a need for periodic blood transfusions, an inability to assimilate red-blood by-products, skin discoloration, and an extreme sensitivity to light. For this reason, even though he was in a deep coma, the lights in my father's room were always kept quite low; the fear was, were he ever to come out of this coma, the shock of all the bright lights would kill him.

Dr. Bennett had an old, tired face. The rings beneath his eyes were like dark brown ruts in a road. He had been our doctor for years, for I don't know how long. But he was a good doctor, and we trusted him.

"I'll tell you," he said to us that night, his hand on my shoulder, our friendship deepening as we watched my father's condition deteriorate. "I want to speak to you candidly now."

He looked at me, then at Mom, and seemed to think it over again before he spoke.

"Mr. Bloom may not make it out of this one," he said.

And my mother and I, almost in unison, said, "I see."

He said, "There are a couple of things we

want to try — we're not giving up, not by a long shot. But I've seen this sort of thing before. It's sad, I — I've known Edward Bloom for a quarter of a century. I don't feel like his doctor anymore. I feel like a friend, you know? A friend who wishes he could do something. But without the machines . . ." Dr. Bennett said, and shook his sad head once, not finishing the sentence, and never starting it with an ending in mind.

I turned and wandered away while he continued to talk to my mother. I went to my father's room and sat in the chair beside his bed. I sat there and waited — for what I don't know — and stared at those marvelous machines. This wasn't life, of course. This was life support. This was what the medical world had fashioned to take the place of Purgatory. I could see how many breaths he was taking by looking at a monitor. I could see what his frenetic heart was up to. And there were a couple of wavy lines and numbers I wasn't sure about at all, but I kept an eye on them as well. In fact, after a while it was the machines I was looking at, not my father at all. They had become him. They were telling me his story.

Which reminds me of this joke. I'll always remember his jokes, but this one especially I will remember. It's a family heirloom. It's one I tell myself still, out loud and alone, the way he told it to me, I say, There's this man. There's this man, and he's a poor man but he needs a new suit. This man needs a new suit but he can't afford to buy one, he can't afford to buy one until he passes a store where there's this suit on sale, and it's priced just right, this beautiful dark blue suit with pinstripes — and so he buys it. Just like that he buys it and wears it right out of the store with a matching tie and everything, but the joke here is — and I guess I should've mentioned this earlier — the joke is it doesn't fit. This suit doesn't fit him at all. It's simply way too big. But it's his suit, right? It's his suit. So to make it look good he has to place an elbow against his side like *this*, and his other arm out sort of like *this*, and he has to walk without moving one of his legs so that the cuffs will appear even, this tiny man in this huge suit — which, as I said, he walks out wearing, walks out into the street wearing. And he thinks to himself, *What a nice suit I have!* and walks with his arms just so — my father would make his arms just so — and dragging one leg behind with this smile on his face like an idiot because of this great buy he's just made — a suit! on sale! — when he passes two old women on the avenue there. They watch him pass, and one of them shakes her head and says to the other, "What a poor, poor man!" And the other woman says, "Yes — but what a nice suit!"

Which is the end of this joke.

But I can't tell it like my father did. I can't drag my leg the way he did it, and so even though this is the funniest joke I have ever heard in my life, I don't laugh. I can't. Even when the lady says "Yes — but what a nice suit!" I'm not laughing. I'm not laughing at all.

I'm doing the other thing.

I suppose this is what roused him, brought him back to the world for a bit, thinking that if there was anytime I needed a joke, now was the time.

God, he really cracked me up.

I look at him and he looks at me.

"Some water," he says to me. "Get me some water."

Some water, he says!

Oh and it's his voice all right, it's his voice, deep and booming, caring and gentle. Mom, bless her heart, is still out talking to the doctor. And I get him some water, and he calls me over, to his bed, his only son, me, his only child, and he pats a place on the edge of the bed where I'm to sit, right? So I sit. There's no time for hellos and how are yous and we both know it. He wakes up and just looks at me in the chair where I am and then he pats a place on his bed where I'm to sit. I sit and he says, after taking a sip of water from the little plastic cup, "Son," he says, "I'm worried."

And he says it in this real shaky voice so I know, don't ask me how but I know that, machines or not, this will be the last time I ever see him alive. Tomorrow, he'll be dead.

And I say, "What is it you're worried about, Dad? The hereafter?"

And he says, "No, dummy. I'm worried about you." He says, "You're an idiot. You couldn't get yourself arrested without me along to help."

But I don't take it personal: he's trying to be funny. He's trying to be funny and *this is the best he can do!* Now I know he's a goner.

And I say, "Don't worry about me, Dad. I'll be okay. I'll be fine."

And he says, "I'm a father, I can't help it. A father worries. I am a father," he says, so I don't miss his point, "and as a father I've tried to teach you a thing or two. I really did try. Maybe I wasn't around so much, but when I was, I tried to teach. So what I want to know is — you think I did a good job?" And as I am opening my mouth to speak he says, "Wait! Don't answer that!" he says, giving a smile his best shot. But it doesn't quite work. He can't really make one anymore. And so he says, he says to me, dying on the bed in front of me, this man — my father — says, "Oh, go on, then. Just tell me before I die. Tell me what it is I've taught you. Tell me everything it is I've taught you about life so I can go ahead and die and so I won't have to worry so much. Just . . . just go ahead and say it."

I look into his gray-blue dying eyes. We're staring at each other, showing each other our last looks, the faces we'll take with us into eternity, and I'm thinking how I wish I knew him better, how I wish we'd had a life together, wishing my father wasn't such a complete and utter goddamn mystery to me, and I say, *"There's this man,"* I say. *"There's this man, and he's a poor man, but he needs a suit, and —"*

Big Fish

And he smiled. Then he cast his gaze around the room, and he winked at me. He winked!

"Let's get out of here," he said in a hoarse whisper.

"Out of here?" I said. "Dad, you're in no condition —"

"There's a fold-up wheelchair in the bathroom," he said. "Wrap a blanket around me. As soon as we get off this hall, we'll be in the clear. But we don't have much time. Hurry, son!"

I did as he asked, I don't know why. I stepped into the bathroom and saw he was right. There was a wheelchair behind the bathroom door, folded up like a child's stroller. I unfolded it and wheeled it to his bed, where I wrapped him with a pale brown blanket, covering his head like a monk's habit. I lifted him, with a disturbing ease, from his bed and into the chair. I had not gotten no stronger in the last few months, but he had become considerably smaller.

"Go for it!" he said.

I opened the door to his room and peeked out into the hallway. I saw Mom at the nurse's desk with Dr. Bennett, wiping her eyes with a tissue and nodding. I pushed my father in the opposite direction. I dared not even look behind me to see if they had spied us. I just pushed him fast, hoping for the best, and when we came to a corner went around it. Only then did I allow myself a backward view.

Nobody.

So far, so good.

"So. Where are we going?" I asked him, catching my breath.

"The elevators," he said, his voice a little bit muffled below the blanket. "The elevator to the lobby to wherever you parked your car. Parking deck?"

"Yes," I said.

"Then take me there," he said. "*Now*. We don't have much time."

The elevator came and I pushed him on. The door closed behind us, and when they opened again I wheeled him out of there with a daredevil's panache, past a host of doctors in green and white, past nurses holding charts giving me sidelong glances and finally staring. Everybody in the lobby paused and stared at us, knowing this wasn't right somehow, but by then I was traveling at such speed that no one had the time to think to stop us. They simply looked at us as though they had seen something odd — and they had, too, odder than they knew. And then we were gone, wheeling toward the parking deck into a cool spring wind.

"Good job," he said.

"Thanks."

"Still need to hurry, though, Will," he said. "I need some water. I need some water bad."

"I have some in the car," I said. "A thermos full."

"More than that," he said and laughed.

"We'll get more," I said.

"I know you will, son," he said. "I know it."

When we got to the car I lifted him out of the wheelchair and placed him in the front seat. I folded the wheelchair and threw it in the back.

"We won't be needing that," he said.

"We won't?" I said.

"Not where we're going," he said, and I thought I heard him laugh again.

But he didn't tell me where we were going, not at first. I simply drove away from everything I knew: the hospital, his old office, home. When I looked at him for a clue he was silent, covered in the blanket.

"That water, William?" he said after a minute.

"Oh," I said. "Here."

It was beside me on the seat. I opened the top and passed it to him. One shaky, scaly hand appeared from beneath the folds and took it from me. But instead of drinking it, he poured it all over himself. The blanket was soaked.

"Ahh," he said. "That's the ticket."

Still, he didn't take the blanket off.

"Go north on Highway 1," he told me, but I had to strain to hear him. His voice was muffled beneath the blanket, and seemed to come from far away.

"North on Highway 1," I said.

"There's a place there," he said. "There's a river. A place by the river."

"*Edward's Grove,*" I said to myself.

And he said, "What?"

"Nothing," I said.

I took the car down a series of streets, through the city and the surrounding suburbs, where the sun was rising over the roofs and treetops, until finally we broke into the deep, green, beautiful country. Suddenly we were surrounded by it: trees and farms and cows and an azure sky, a home for clouds and the occasional bird. I'd been out this way, once before.

"How far now?" I asked him.

"Just a couple more miles, I think," he said.

"I *hope*. I don't feel so good."

"What's there?" I asked, but for an answer all I got was a shivering inside the damp blanket, and a gurgling, groaning sound, as if he were in deep pain.

"Are you okay?" I asked.

"Been better," he said. "I feel like that guy . . ."

Who walks into the bar with a frog on his head, with a bird on his shoulder, with a kangaroo at his side and the bartender says, "Hey, we don't get that many kangaroos in here," and the kangaroo says, "Yeah, and at these prices you're not likely to get many more!"

And then he said, suddenly almost yelling, "Here!"

And I pulled off the road.

It wasn't Edward's Grove as far as I know, but it might as well have been. There was your old oak tree with the roots spreading out through the dark and mossy soil. There were your rhododendrons. There was your rabbit, hopping away at a leisurely gait, eyeing us with a backward glance. And there was your river, running clear the way you didn't think rivers ran anymore, moving fast around stones the size of a small car, making little rapids, running as clear as the air, as blue as the sky, as white as a cloud.

I don't know how he saw it from beneath the blanket.

"Carry me," he said, or so it sounded, his voice so weak now I was doing my share of interpreting as I listened. He said, *Carry me* and *You don't know how I appreciate what you're doing* and *When you see your mother, tell her — tell her I said good-bye.* And so I carried him out of the car and down the mossy bank to the river and stood there before it, holding my father in my arms. And I knew what I was supposed to do then but I couldn't do it. I just stood there, holding his body shrouded in a blanket on the banks of this river, until he told me, *You might want to look away now* and then *Please,* and all of a sudden my arms were full of the most fantastic life, frenetic, impossible to hold on to even if I'd wanted to, and I wanted to. But then all I was holding was the blanket, because my father had jumped into the river. And that's when I discovered that my father hadn't been dying after all. He was just changing, transforming himself into something new and different to carry his life forward in.

All this time, my father was becoming a fish.

I saw him dart this way and that, a silvery, brilliant, shining life, and disappear into the darkness of the deep water where the big fish go, and I haven't seen him since — though others have. Already I've heard stories, of lives saved and wishes granted, of children carried for miles on his back, of anglers mischievously dumped from their vessels and emptied into various oceans and streams from Beaufort to Hyannis by the biggest fish they've ever seen, and they tell their stories to anybody who will listen.

But no one believes them. No one believes a word.